DEATH IN THE
FIFTH POSITION

Mr Edgar Box is a light, fluent writer, very
readable, very amusing.

TIMES LITERARY SUPPLEMENT

Sprightly, hypersophisticated little murder
mystery.

OBSERVER

A lively story . . . a witty and urbane tale.

DAILY TELEGRAPH

Death in the Fifth Position

EDGAR BOX

A FOUR SQUARE BOOK

First published, in Great Britain, by William Heinemann Ltd., in 1954
Published in an Ace Books edition in 1960

*

FIRST FOUR SQUARE EDITION 1965

*Four Square Books are published by The New English Library Limited from Barnard's
Inn, Holborn, London, E.C.1. Made and Printed in Great Britain by Hunt Barnard & Co.
Limited, The Sign of the Dolphin, Aylesbury, Buckinghamshire.*

I

'You see,' said Mr. Washburn. 'We've been having trouble.'

I nodded. 'What sort of trouble?'

He looked vaguely out the window. 'Oh, one thing and the other.'

'That's not much to go on, is it?' I said gently; it never does to be stern with a client before one is formally engaged.

'Well, there's the matter of these pickets.'

I don't know why but the word 'picket' at this moment suggested small gnomes hiding in the earth. So I said, 'Ah.'

'They are coming tonight,' he added.

'What time do they usually come?' I asked, getting into the spirit of the thing.

'I don't know. We've never had them before.'

Never had them before, I wrote in my notebook, just to be doing something.

'You were very highly recommended to me,' said Mr. Washburn, in a tone which was almost accusing; obviously I had given him no cause for confidence.

'I've handled a few big jobs, from time to time,' I said quietly, exuding competence.

'I want you for the rest of the season, the New York season. You are to handle all our public relations, except for the routine stuff which this office does automatically: sending out photographs of the dancers and so on. Your job will be to work with the columnists, that kind of thing . . . to see we're not smeared.'

'Why do you think you might be smeared?' The psychological moment had come for a direct question.

'The pickets,' said Mr. Washburn with a sigh. He was a tall heavy man with a bald pink head which glittered as though it had been waxed; his eyes were grey and shifty: as all honest men's eyes are supposed to be according to those psychologists who maintain that there is nothing quite so dishonest as a level, unwavering gaze.

5

I finally understood him. 'You mean you are going to be picketed?'

'That's what I said.'

'Bad labor relations?'

'Communism.'

'You mean the Communists are going to picket you?'

The impresario of the Grand Saint Petersburg Ballet looked at me sadly, as though once again his faith had been unjustified. Then he began at the beginning. 'I called you over here this morning because I was told that you were one of the best of the younger public relations men in New York, and I prefer to work with young people. As you may or may not know, my company is going to première an important new ballet tonight. The first major modern ballet we have presented in many years and the choreographer is a man named Jed Wilbur.'

'I'm a great admirer of his,' I said, just to show that I knew something about ballet. As a matter of fact, it isn't possible to be around the theater and not know of Wilbur. He is the hottest choreographer in town at the moment, the most fashionable . . . not only in ballet but also in musical comedies.

'Wilbur has been accused of being a Communist several times but since he has already been cleared by two boards I have every confidence in him. The United Veterans Committee, however, have not. They wired me yesterday that if we did his new ballet they would picket every performance until it was withdrawn.'

'That's bad,' I said, frowning, making it sound worse than it was: after all I had a good job at stake. 'May I see their telegram?' Mr. Washburn handed it to me and I read:

To Ivan Washburn Director Grand Saint Petersburg Ballet Company Metropolitan Opera House New York City: WE HAVE REASON TO BELIEVE THAT JED WILBUR IS A MEMBER OF THE COMMUNIST PARTY AND THAT COMMA TO PROTECT OUR CHERISHED WAY OF LIFE AND THOSE IDEALS WHICH SO FINELY FORGED A NATION OUT OF THE WILDERNESS COMMA THE SUBVERSIVE WORK OF ARTISTS LIKE WILBUR SHOULD BE BANNED PERIOD SHOULD YOU DISREGARD THIS PLEA TO PROTECT OUR AMERICAN WAY WE WILL BE FORCED TO PICKET EVERY PERFORMANCE OF SAID WILBUR'S WORK PERIOD IN A TRUE DEMOCRACY THERE IS NO PLACE FOR A DIFFERENCE OF OPINION ON GREAT ISSUES CORDIALLY ABNER S. FLEER SECRETARY.

'A poignant composition,' I said.

'We've had a bad season so far this year. We're the fifth ballet company to arrive in town this spring and even though we're the original Russian ballet it's not been easy to fill the Met. Wilbur is our ace-in-the-hole. It's his first ballet for this company. It's his first new work in over a year. Everyone is going to be on hand tonight . . . and *nothing* must go wrong. That will be your job, too, by the way: to publicize the première.'

'If I'd had a few weeks of preparation I could have got *Life* to cover the performance,' I said with that modesty which characterizes my profession.

Washburn was not impressed. 'In any case, I'm told that you've got a good many contacts among the columnists. They're the people who make opinion, for us at least. You've got to convince them that Wilbur is as pure as . . .'

'The driven snow,' I finished, master that I am of the worn cliché. 'But is he?'

'Is he what?'

'Pure as . . . I mean is he a Communist?'

'How in the name of God should I know? He could be an anarchist for all I care. The only thing I am interested in is a successful season. Besides, what has politics to do with *Eclipse*?'

'With what?'

'*Eclipse* is the name of the new ballet. I want you to go over to the Met and watch the dress rehearsal at two-thirty. You'll be able to get some idea of the company then . . . meet the cast and so on. Meet Wilbur, too; he's full of ideas on how to handle this . . . too damn many ideas.'

'Then I am officially employed?'

'As of this minute . . . for the rest of the season, two weeks altogether. If we're still having trouble by the time we go on tour I'd like you to go with us as far as Chicago . . . if that's agreeable.'

'We'll see,' I said.

'Fine.' Mr. Washburn rose and so did I. 'You'll probably want to make some preparations between now and two-thirty. You can use the office next to mine . . . Miss Ruger will show you which one.'

'That will be perfect,' I said. We shook hands solemnly.

I was halfway out the door when Mr. Washburn said, 'I think I should warn you that ballet dancers are very tempera-

7

mental people. Don't take them too seriously. Their little quarrels are always a bit louder than life.' Which, in the light of what happened later, was something of an understatement.

2

Until my interview with Ivan Washburn I could take ballet or leave it alone and since in earlier days I was busy writing theater reviews for Milton Haddock of the *New York Globe*, I left it alone: besides, the music critic always handled ballet and what with doing Mr. Haddock's work as well as my own I had very little time for that sort of thing, between eight-thirty and eleven anyway. Mr. Haddock, God knows, is a fine critic and a finer man and it is a fact that his reviews in the *Globe* were more respected than almost anyone else's; they should have been since I wrote nearly all of them between 1947 and 1949 at which latter date I was separated from the *Globe*, as we used to say in the army. Not that I am implying Mr. Haddock, who was writing about the theater the year I was born, couldn't do just as well as I did . . . he could, but there is a limit to the amount of work you can accomplish on Scotch whisky, taken without water or ice, directly from the bottle if he was in the privacy of his office or from a discreet prohibition flask if we were at the theater: he on the aisle fifth row from the stage and I just behind him in the sixth row, with instructions to poke the back of his neck if he snored too loud.

In a way, I had a perfect setup; Mr. Haddock was fond of me in a distant fatherly way (he often had a struggle recalling my name) and I was allowed all the pleasure of unedited authorship for he never changed a line of my reviews on those occasions when he read them at all. The absence of public credit never distressed me; after all I was Harvard class of 1946 (three years must be added to my age, however, during which time I served the nation on at least one very far-flung battlefront) and most of my classmates are still struggling along in the lower echelons of advertising firms or working anonymously for *Time* and *Life* and worrying about their integrity as liberals in a capitalistic organization. Anyway I knew a good thing when I saw it but after three years of being the real drama critic for the *Globe* I began to feel my oats and I made the mistake of asking for a raise at the wrong time: a fault in timing which must be ascribed to my extreme youth and natural arrogance, to quote Mr. Haddock quoting the managing editor, and since I had unfortunately phrased my request as an ultimatum I was forced to resign and Mr. Haddock looked very sorry and confused the day I left, saying: 'All the best, Jim.' My name is Peter Cutler Sargeant II, but what the hell; I shook his hand and told him that everything I knew about writing I had learned from him . . . which pleased the old fool.

For over a year now I have been in public relations, with my own office, consisting of a middle-aged lady and a filing cabinet. The middle-aged lady, Miss Flynn, is my official conscience and she has been very good to me, reminding me that money is not everything and that Jesus is my redeemer. She is a Baptist and stern in the presence of moral weakness. I firmly believe that the main reason she consents to work for me is that I constitute a challenge to her better instincts, to that evangelical spirit which burns secretly but brightly in her bosom. She will save me yet. We have both accepted that fact. But in the meantime she helps me in my work, quite unaware that she is a party to that vast conspiracy to dupe the public in which I and my kind are eternally engaged.

'Miss Flynn, I have been hired.'

'The dancers?' She looked at me, her grey lips tight. Women in tights are dancers to her, not ballerinas.

'For two weeks, starting now.'

'I am very happy for you, Mr. Sargeant,' she said, in the tone of one bidding a friend farewell on the banks of the Styx.

'I'm happy, too,' I said. I then gave her a few instructions about my other accounts (a hat company in the Bronx, a television actress and a night school); then I left my one-room Madison Avenue office and headed for the Metropolitan Opera House, leaving my conscience behind.

Mr. Washburn met me at the stage door and escorted me past several open dressing rooms to a flight of steps which led down to the vast stage itself. Everything was in great confusion. Small fat women ran back and forth carrying costumes, while dancers in tights stood about practising difficult variations with the intensely vacuous expressions of weight-lifters or of those restaurant cooks who scramble eggs in front of plate-glass windows. Workmen, carrying parts of scenery, shouted to one another

9

and cursed the dancers who seemed always to be in their way. In the pit the orchestra was making an awful noise warming up, while, beyond, the great red and gold opera house was empty and still . . . a little ominous, I thought, for no reason at all.

'The rehearsal is almost ready to begin,' said my employer as we moved out on to the stage, toward a group of dancers in tights and T-shirts, the standard rehearsal costume of both boys and girls, which was very nice I thought, looking at the girls. 'I'll introduce you to the principals in a minute,' said Mr. Washburn. 'If you . . .' But then someone waved to him from the other side of the stage and he walked away, leaving his sentence unfinished.

'Are you a new boy?' asked a female voice behind me.

I turned and saw a very pretty girl standing behind me; she wore black tights and a white T-shirt through which her breasts showed, small and neat. She was combing her dark gold hair back. For some inscrutable reason she had a rubber band in her mouth; it impaired her diction.

'Well, I guess in a way I am,' I said.

'You better get your clothes off. I'm Jane Garden.'

'My name's Peter Sargeant.'

'You better hurry. You've got to learn the whole thing this afternoon.' She pulled her hair straight back and then slipped the back hair through the rubber band; it looked like a horse's tail, a very nice horse's tail.

'Shall I take them off right here?'

'Don't be silly. The boys' dressing room is on the second floor.'

I then explained to her who I was and she giggled, but not in a squeaky manner: her voice was low and her eyes, I noticed, were a fine arctic blue.

'Do you know *anything* about ballet?' she asked, glancing anxiously toward the other dancers. They were not ready, however. The orchestra was still warming up. The principals hadn't arrived yet. The noise was deafening.

'Not much,' I said. 'Are you one of the leads?'

'Nowhere near being a lead. Although they've made me understudy in this ballet.'

'To whom?'

'Why, to Ella Sutton. She's the star of the ballet . . . I mean

of this particular one. Actually she's the second-ranking ballerina . . . after Eglanova.'

I knew who Eglanova was. Everyone, I suspect, who has ever
heard of ballet knows about Anna Eglanova. I had even read
up on her that morning before my interview with Mr. Washburn, just so I wouldn't appear too ignorant. The program
notes and the facts, however, did not coincide as I found out
soon enough . . . even though the program is approximately
correct; she *was* a star at the same time as Nijinski and she
is a genuine Russian dancer from the Old Imperial School,
but she is fifty-one not thirty-eight and she has been married
five times, not once, and she was not the greatest ballerina of
the Diaghilev era; as a matter of fact she was considered the
least promising of the lot: how were her contemporaries to
know that she had joints like ball bearings and a pair of lungs
like rubber water wings and that with this equipment she would
outlive all her generation, existing finally as a legend whose
appearance on a stage was enough to break up a whole audience,
causing tears of nostalgia to come to the eyes of characters who
never saw a ballet before the last war.

'Where is Sutton?' I asked.

'Over there, talking to Wilbur . . . in the wings.'

Sutton was a good-looking woman, with hair dyed jetblack
and worn severely combed back with a part in the middle: the
classic ballerina fashion. She had large but good features and a
vividly painted face; she was in costume, a full-skirted white
dress with red roses in her hair. Her body was good for a female
dancer though the muscles tended to bunch a little unpleasantly
at the calves. Jane Garden's did not, I noticed.

'Why aren't you in costume?' I asked. 'Isn't this the dress
rehearsal?'

'My costume isn't ready. I wish they'd hurry up and start.'

'Why don't they?'

'I suppose they're waiting for Louis . . . Louis Giraud, he's the
first dancer and he's always late. He sleeps most of the time.
It drives everyone crazy . . . especially Wilbur.'

'Why doesn't he do something about it?'

'Who? Wilbur? Why, he's in love.'

'In love?'

'Of course . . . everybody knows it. He's just crazy about
Louis.'

11

Well, this is ballet, I decided, making a mental note to keep Miss Flynn in complete darkness as to the character of my new associates.

'I wonder,' I said thoughtfully, sincerely, 'if you might perhaps have a minute after the show tonight . . . we might go somewhere and have something to eat. You see' (speaking quickly now, gathering momentum), 'I have to learn an awful lot about ballet very fast. It would help if you were to explain it all to me.'

'You're sweet,' said Miss Garden with an unexpected smile, her teeth shone glacier-white in her warm pink face. 'Maybe I will. Oh, here comes the conductor. You better get out of the way now . . . we're going to start.'

Mr. Washburn collected me at that moment and we went around to the front of the house. Here I was introduced to a number of patrons and hangers-on, as well as the *regisseur* or director of the company, Alyosha Rudin, a nice old man, and the set designer whose name I didn't get.

Jed Wilbur, a thin, prematurely grey young man, came out on stage and began to lecture the dancers in a high nasal voice. They looked very pretty I thought. The girls in grey with pink roses in their hair and the boys dressed like 1910. But all was not ready.

'Where's Louis?' asked Wilbur suddenly. 'Doesn't he know this is dress rehearsal?'

'He's always late,' said Ella, fixing one of her false eyelashes in place. 'I suppose he's sleeping.'

'Just resting my legs,' said Louis, ambling out on to the stage with that funny duck-like walk all dancers have from continually turning their feet out. He was a big-boned man, about thirty and, for a dancer, rather tall and muscular, with black curly hair and blue eyes.

'Why can't you ever be on time?' complained Wilbur, the eye of love eclipsed by the great love of art and reputation; this was obviously an important moment for him, a major work . . . all the critics would be out front tonight and maybe even Margaret Truman.

'I get here, Jed. Now you start.' Ella glared at him. Wilbur muttered something disagreeable. Then the overture began.

The set was a handsome one. A blue sky, which was dark when the curtain rose, gradually filled with light as the music swelled and the *corps de ballet* (eight boys and eight girls) appeared. In the center of the stage was a large rock of grey canvas while at the top of the blue sky, about forty feet up, was a yellow Van Gogh sun.

The plot, if *Eclipse* could be said to have a plot, seemed to be about a girl (Sutton) who was in love with a boy (Louis) who liked all the girls in the company except her. So, frustrated and miserable, she took her revenge when, not having been laid as she so dearly wanted, she rushed furiously away from the happy boys and girls who at this point were indulging in some pretty sophisticated fornication on stage (so stylized, however, that one's grandmother would never suspect what was happening); for a few dozen bars Ella hid behind the rock while Louis did his solo. Then, when he was finished, she reappeared and with a look of sheer malevolence slowly ascended into the air, spinning like an avenging spirit until she had at last eclipsed the sun. It was quite a tour de force, I thought . . . in spite of the dress rehearsal which was sufficiently godawful to make everyone think that tonight's performance would be a technical triumph: Louis dropped Ella in the midst of a complicated lift shortly after her entrance and they never got back with the music again, while the *corps de ballet* plunged wildly about in the best St. Petersburg tradition, knocking into scenery and one another, justifying all the cruel remarks I'd heard made about them by the more refined balletomanes.

'What do you think?' asked Washburn when the rehearsal ended.

'Wonderful!' I said, like a press agent.

'I think . . .' began Mr. Washburn, but he was not allowed to finish because they were having a row on stage. The curtain had remained up and the lights were on again. Louis, stretched out with his back to the proscenium, was carefully wiping the sweat from his face with a piece of Kleenex. The boys and girls stood puffing at the rear of the stage while Ella and Wilbur quarrelled.

'You've got to change it, Jed. I insist. I will *not* go sailing up on that damn thing again.'

'It's the whole point to the ballet.'

'So what? I won't do it. I get dizzy and I can't make those turns off the ground.'

'We can have one of the workmen turn you backstage . . . he'll jerk the cable . . .'

'Oh, no he won't!'

'The idea never seemed to bother you before.'

'The *idea* still doesn't bother me. I never realized how high it was until now.'

'Why don't you get her a net?' suggested Louis.

'And that lift!' she said furiously, turning on him. 'I could have broken a leg. You did it deliberately. I *swear* he dropped me deliberately.'

Mr. Washburn let them fight it out a few minutes more; then he went up on the stage, accompanied by me, and quickly made peace. It was agreed that Ella *would* ascend by cable tonight, but more slowly than before, and, further, she would not have to turn in the air.

'Very statesmanlike,' I said to Mr. Washburn, as we moved toward the dressing rooms on the north side of the stage.

'We always have these little disagreements before a première . . . divertissements I like to call them.' Despite his attempt at lightness, however, he seemed not at all diverted. 'Have you had any ideas yet about those pickets?'

I nodded. 'I've already called Elmer Bush at the *Globe* . . . that's where I used to work . . . and he's doing a column called "Witch-Hunt in the Theater", all about Wilbur and the ballet.'

'First-rate,' said Mr. Washburn, obviously impressed. I made a mental note to call Elmer Bush and suggest such a column to him. For all I knew he might even do it.

'I would rather wait until after we see the pickets before I do anything more. I mean we may get a lead from them . . . you know, something about bad behavior, bullying is un-American, that kind of thing. By the way,' I added, 'speaking of bad behavior, does Miss Sutton often make scenes like this?'

'Not often,' said Mr. Washburn, as we approached a dressing room with a dusty star on the door. 'She usually saves them for her husband.'

'Her husband?'

'Miles Sutton. He's the conductor . . . big fellow with the beard.'

My head was beginning to spin. Everyone was related to everyone else, either officially or unofficially. I couldn't keep them straight. The ballerina Ella Sutton was the wife of the conductor Miles Sutton and the choreographer Jed Wilbur was in love with the lead dancer Louis Giraud and Jane Garden the understudy to Ella Sutton was my idea of a fine specimen while Anna Eglanova the prima ballerina stood before me naked from the waist up. It was disconcerting. I was standing beside Mr. Washburn in the doorway of her dressing room; her maid had suddenly opened the door and darted by, leaving her mistress exposed to our gaze.

'Come in, Ivan,' said the great ballerina. 'Who is the young man?'

'Peter Sargeant, Anna, our new public relations man.'

'So young! Ah!' She sat down before her dressing table and began to arrange her hair. She looked young for fifty. Her body was firm . . . the skin like antique ivory and the breasts more like worn china door knobs than glands intended for the suckling of the young. Her neck was slightly corded and her face was ugly but exotic, with deep lines about the mouth, a beaked nose and narrow slanting Mongol eyes. Her hair was dyed dark red.

'I get ready now for *pas de deux*, Ivan.' Her English was so heavily accented that it sounded to me like a different language altogether. In fact everything about her was different, including her casual disregard for the conventions.

'I think I better go,' I said, a little hastily. 'I've got some calls to make. I'm going to try and head the newspaper photographers off.'

'Good plan,' said Mr. Washburn.

'Nice boy,' said Anna, as I left.

Halfway down the hall, a loud voice said, 'Hey, Baby, come in here.'

Now I am twenty-eight years old and shave every day of my life and, though I wear a crewcut in deference to my collegiate past, I flatter myself that I look every inch a man of the world. But Louis Giraud obviously had about as much respect for other men as Don Juan had for little girls so I controlled myself. I walked into his dressing room.

He was lying on a steel cot. He had an electric fan going just above his head and a pair of sweaty tights were hanging over the radiator to dry. He wore nothing except a towel around his middle.

I said, 'Hi.'

'You like the ballet tonight?' He spoke good English with

15

only a faint French accent; he had started life as a longshoreman in Marseille. No one knew how he had got started in ballet but I suspect that the rumor a certain rich gentleman discovered him in a bordello and took him to Paris was probably true.

'I liked it pretty good,' I said.

'Real lousy,' said Louis, stretching his long knotty legs until the joints cracked. 'I hate this ugly modern stuff. *Giselle* was good enough for Nijinski and it's good enough for me. All these people running around stage with funny faces. *Merde!*' He had a deep voice and he wasn't at all like the other boys in the company who were inclined to be rather tender: Louis had shoulders like a boxer. I decided I wouldn't like to tangle with him and so I sat near the open door, ready to make a quick exit if he should decide to tear off a quick piece.

'Well, it's a new medium,' I said absently, noting the comic books and movie magazines on the floor by the bed. Each to his taste, I said to myself in flawless French.

'But it's not ballet.' Louis looked at me and grinned. 'Hey, why're you trying to fool me, Baby?'

I measured the distance from my chair to the door: two long steps or one broad jump, I decided coolly. 'Who's trying to fool you?' I asked, getting up slowly with a look of innocence which would have done credit to Tom Sawyer. He was too quick for me, though. I made a leap for the door but he got there first. It was a very silly moment.

'Now, look here, Louis,' I said as he made a grab for me. We played tag a moment and then he grabbed me, holding me the way a boxer holds another boxer in a clinch and both of us trying not to make any noise, for different reasons. I wondered whether to knee him or not; the towel had fallen off. I decided against it for the good of the company. I would be fired if I did. On the other hand I was in danger of being ravished; I couldn't move without seriously injuring him and, on the other, I couldn't stand like this forever pressed against his front while he fumbled and groped with his one free hand, embarrassing me very much. He smelled like a horse. Controlling myself with great effort I said in a very even and dignified voice, 'If you don't let go of me, I will break every one of your toes.' And with that, fairly gently, I put one hard leather heel on top of his left foot. He jumped at that and, breathing hard, I slid out the door.

16

I was mad as hell for several minutes but then, since no damage was done, I began to see the funny side and as I walked across the stage to the other set of dressing rooms I wondered if I should tell Jane what had happened. For one reason and another I had decided not to when I came upon Miles and Ella Sutton, quarrelling. He was standing in the door of her dressing room; she was sitting at her make-up table in an old grey bathrobe. I caught one quick glimpse of her as I walked by, as though on urgent business. I have found that people who hang around to watch fights usually end by getting involved.

As I walked by, however, I heard Miles Sutton threatening to kill his wife. It gave me quite a turn. I mean temperament is all very well but there are times when it can be carried too far.

3

Now that I look back on that night it is perfectly apparent to me that almost everyone, including myself, sensed that something serious had gone wrong . . . but what? I knew of course that there was always a great deal of tension before a première and the childish bad temper of ballet dancers was familiar to me, by reputation anyway. Yet when the curtain went up on the blue-lit stage for the first ballet of the evening, *Swan Lake*, I had a knot in the pit of my stomach.

I remember taking a good look at the audience just before the house lights were dimmed and I remember feeling thankful that I didn't have to appear on a stage in front of all those people, for the interior of the Met, seen from the stage, is like the mouth of a great monster, wide open, yawning and red, with tiers of golden teeth.

I have always had a personal superstition that when something begins badly it will end well and vice versa. Since that night I have discarded the superstition of a lifetime for this particular evening began badly and ended tragically.

The pickets arrived at seven-thirty, twenty well-fed veterans of the First World War; they were quiet but grim and their placards suggested in red ink that Wilbur go back to Russia if he liked it so much there. I had already telephoned the photographers, tipping them off; all publicity is good is my conviction and I had a scheme by which we might eventually be able to make considerable capital out of the veterans. Mr. Washburn took a dark view of this but I reassured him. I even wrote him a little speech to make to the audience right after *Swan Lake*, before *Eclipse*, saying that Jed Wilbur was a hundred per cent patriot and so on.

The trouble began, officially, after *Swan Lake* when one of the girls collapsed in the wings and had to be carried up to her dressing room.

I was standing beside Alyosha Rudin to stage right when this happened.

'What's the matter with her?' I asked.

The old man sighed. 'A foolish girl. Her name is Magda . . . a little heavy to be good dancer but she has the heart.'

'You mean she has a weak heart?'

Alyosha chuckled. 'No, she is passionate. Shall we go out front?'

On our way we passed Mr. Washburn. He was dressed in white tie and tails and his glittering skull looked pale to me in the dim light of backstage. He was very nervous. 'I don't think I'll be able to go through with it,' he said in a voice which trembled.

'With what?' I asked.

'The curtain speech.'

'Courage, Ivan,' said Alyosha. 'You always say that; then when the time comes, you have the courage of a lion.'

'All those people,' moaned Mr. Washburn, moving toward the lavatory.

Alyosha was a pleasant companion and most knowledgeable of ballet; as he should be since, like Eganova, he is a genuine Russian dating back to the Fall of Rome . . . perhaps even to the pyramids for he is very old with the classic Russian greyhound head: hair brushed back, long features and eyes like grey metal. He looked very old-world and distinguished in a smoking jacket of mulberry velvet. We found ourselves two seats in the front row.

'What was wrong with that girl?' I asked when we were seated. Already I was beginning to think of a press release . . . dancer upset by pickets: lover killed in Korea.

'She will have baby,' said Alyosha.

'But she shouldn't be dancing if she's pregnant.'

18

'The poor child. She must. She has no husband and her family doesn't know.'

'Do you know who the father is?'

Alyosha smiled sadly; his teeth were like black pearls. 'Sometimes it doesn't matter,' he said gently.

Then the house lights were turned down and Mr. Washburn made his curtain speech; there was polite applause. Miles Sutton, looking nervous and sick, I thought (we were sitting right behind him), rapped his baton sharply on the music stand and the ballet began.

Artistically, everything went off quite well, according to the critics the next day. Both Martin of the *Times* and Terry of the *Tribune* thought *Eclipse* a triumphant modern work, praising Wilbur, Sutton's interpretation of the Bartok music, the set designer, Louis and, above all, the ballerina Ella Sutton who, they both felt, gave her finest performance: a dedicated artist to the very end for, when the cable broke thirty odd feet in the air, she maintained complete silence as she fell in fifth position on to the stage with a loud crash, still on beat.

Alyosha who was sitting beside me, gasped and said something very loud in Russian; then he crossed himself as the curtain swept down over the stage and the house lights went on. The audience was too stunned to react. Mr. Washburn came on stage but I missed his announcement for I was already backstage.

Ella Sutton lay in a heap in the middle of the stage, her body curiously twisted, like a contortionist's. A doctor had been summoned and he was kneeling beside her, his hand on her pulse. The dancers stood in shocked attitudes around the still figure.

Then Ella was pronounced dead (her back was broken) and she was carried to her dressing room. Alyosha ordered the dancers to change for the next ballet, *Scheherazade*. Mr. Washburn led the doctor away. The impassive workmen struck the set and I suddenly found that I was alone on the stage. Not even Alyosha was in sight.

I wandered down the corridor which led to the north side dressing rooms, but I could find no one. I paused at Eglanova's room and looked in. It was empty. Everything was in a tangle: costumes, telegrams, press clippings, flowers fresh and dying, all the paraphernalia of stardom. On impulse, I entered, feeling like a small boy who has been deserted in a haunted house.

I knew, if I waited long enough, that she'd reappear: her dressing room was the clubhouse of the ballet . . . at least of the top echelon who, I was told, usually came here to drink hot tea and lemon Russian style and discuss, with some severity, those not present. But the club was deserted. Not even Eglanova's maid was in sight.

A little worried, I turned to go when, quite by chance, I glanced at the wastepaper basket which stood just inside the door: something glittered underneath the make-up-stained pieces of Kleenex and the dead roses. I bent over and picked up a large pair of brand-new shears.

I have since tried, unsuccessfully, to recall what I thought at that moment. As far as I can recollect I thought, rather idly, that it was curious that a perfectly good set of shears should be thrown out like that, and in Eglanova's dressing room, too. I had perhaps some vague notion that her maid might have borrowed them from one of the grips and then had absently thrown them out. In any event, I took them out of the dressing room and placed them neatly on top of a tool chest near the north side entrance.

It wasn't until an hour later, after the performance was over, that I began to worry a little because, by that time, the assistant district attorney had arrived, accompanied by a medical examiner and a detective named Gleason who announced to the assembled company that someone had deliberately cut all but a strand of that wire cable with a pair of shears, or maybe a saw, and that Ella Sutton had been murdered.

The company was kept backstage until nearly dawn. The questioning was conducted by Gleason, an autocratic little man who forbade me to call the Press until the first of what proved to be a long set of interviews was concluded.

4

We met, almost by accident on Seventh Avenue at four-thirty in the morning. She looked very demure, I thought, in a plain cotton dress, and carrying a briefcase which contained her ballet clothes. I stopped beside her on the corner and we both waited for the light to turn green. Lonely taxicabs hurtled by; the city was still and a grey light shone dull in the east, above the granite and steel peaks, beyond the slow river.

'Hello, Jane,' I said.

For a moment she didn't recognize me; then, remembering, she smiled wanly, and her face pale by street lamp, she said, 'Are you going to take me out to dinner?'

'What about breakfast?'

'I never get up this early,' she said; and we crossed the street. The light was green. A sudden gust of warm wind came bowling up the alley and I caught her scent as Edgar Rice Burroughs was wont to say: warm flesh and Ivory soap.

'Can I walk you home?' I asked.

'If you want to. I live on Second Avenue.' We walked nine uptown blocks and seven crosstown blocks to the brownstone where she lived. We paused below in the street . . . the hot wind, redolent of summer and river and early morning, stirred her streaked blonde hair as we stood before a delicatessen while the drama of courtship took place. The dialogue, I must admit, was similar to that of every other couple in this same predicament at this same hour in the quiet city. Should we or should we not? was the moon right? and was this wise? or was it love? Fortunately, being a well-trained girl of casual habits, this last point wasn't worried too much and at last we walked up the two flights to her apartment.

The dialogue continued as, both seated on a studio couch in her two-roomed apartment, we were momentarily diverted from my central interest by the murder and, though we were both dead-tired and stifling yawns heroically in deference to my lust, we talked of the death of Ella Sutton.

'I never thought such a thing could happen to anybody I knew,' said Jane, lying back on the bed, a pillow under her head. One paper lantern illuminated the room with red and yellow light. The furniture was shabby Victorian, very homelike, with photographs of family and fellow dancers on the walls, over the mantel of the walled-up fireplace. The ceilings were high and the curtains were of faded red plush.

'Do you think it was really murder?'

'That awful little man certainly thought it was. Somebody cut the cable . . . that's what he said.'

'I wonder who?'

21

'Oh, almost anybody,' she said vaguely, scratching her stomach comfortably.

'Don't tell me now that *everybody* hated Ella . . . it would be much too pat.'

'Well, almost everybody did. Oh, she was just terrible. But that's an awful thing to say . . . her being dead, I mean.'

'I expect we'll be hearing a lot about how terrible she was,' I said, moving closer to her on the couch, my cup of tea in my hand (tea was the fiction we had both agreed upon to bring us together).

'Well, she wasn't that awful,' said Jane, in the tone of one who wants to think only good of others. 'I suppose she had her nice side.' Then she gave up. 'God knows what it was, though. I never saw it.'

'Perhaps God *does* know,' I said, rolling my eyes upward. Jane sighed. I moved closer, the teacup rattling in my hand.

'She was such a schemer,' said Jane thoughtfully. 'She was conniving every minute of the day. That was why she married Miles . . . he was the conductor and very important to the company. So she married him and then lo and behold she began to get some leads . . . though the marriage was always a farce.'

'Didn't she like him?'

'Of course not . . . and after the first few months he was on to her, too. Only she'd never let him get a divorce. He was too useful to her, a perfect front . . .'

'And then he killed her.'

Jane shuddered. 'Don't even think it,' she said in a low voice. 'He's so wonderful . . . I mean as a conductor; I don't know him very well outside the theater. Anyway he's a nice man and Ella was a bitch and I see no reason for him to get in trouble on her account,' she concluded spiritedly, disregarding all ethics in her emotional summary.

'I suppose he's the likeliest suspect,' I said. I was curious about the whole affair, as anyone would be. It was an unusual experience to be involved in a murder during one's first day on a new job. Yet, aside from the novelty of my situation, it had occurred to me dimly that some end might be served by this event, that I might somehow be able to make use of this tragedy, an ignoble sentiment certainly but then I belong to an ignoble tribe which trades on the peculiarities and talents of others, even on their disasters.

'I guess so,' said Jane unhappily. 'Lord knows he hated her. On the other hand so did a lot of people. Eglanova, for instance.'

'Why? What did she have against Ella?'

'Don't you know?' And for the first time (but not the last) I received that pitying dancer's glance which implied that though I might not be entirely a square I was none the less hopelessly ignorant of all that really mattered: the dance and its intricate politics. I said I didn't know, humbly.

'Mr. Washburn was all set to fire Eglanova this year. She's practically blind, you know. It's got so even the audience notices it . . . why they even applaud her when she finishes a pirouette in the right direction . . . then she's always losing her partner in *Giselle*. She's lucky she's got Louis. He adores her and he follows her around on stage like a Saint Bernard. If she had any other partner she'd've ended up among the violins in the orchestra pit long ago.'

'So Washburn was going to get rid of her?'

'I should say so. Only he acted as though she were retiring of her own free will. We were to end this season at the Met with a Gala Eglanova Evening, to celebrate her thirty-one years as a star; only now . . . well, I suppose she'll have to do the next season. You see, Ella was all set to take her place.'

'Can't they get somebody else?'

Jane looked as incredulous as any girl can at five in the morning after a tough night's performance and a questioning by the police. 'You don't seem to realize that this is the oldest ballet company in the world and that it has to have a *prima ballerina assoluta* and there's only a half dozen of those in the world and they're all engaged like Markova, Fonteyn, Danilova, Toumanova, Alonso . . . or else too expensive for Mr. Washburn,' she added, deflating somewhat the pretensions of the Grand Saint Petersburg Ballet. I knew already, from personal experience, that Mr. Washburn was a tight man with a dollar.

'So Eglanova might have cut that cable?' The memory of those shears still bothered me; I tried to think of something else . . . I had not yet mentioned finding them to the police . . . or to anyone.

'Oh, don't be silly,' said Jane. But she had no other comment to make about this theory.

'She must've been awfully ambitious,' I said sleepily; my eyes beginning to twitch with fatigue.

'Ella? Oh, I'll say she was. She wanted to do *Swan Lake* at the Met on opening night . . . instead of on Wednesday matinees and every night in all cities with a population under a hundred thousand. And she would've too.'

'Was she that good?' It was hopeless to ask one dancer about the talents of another but I was thinking of something else now. I paid no attention to what we were saying. My hand was now on top of hers and I was so close to her that I could feel through my own body the quickened beating of her heart.

Jane told me very seriously that Ella had been a good actress and a good technician but that she had always been remarkably unmusical and that if she had not been married to the conductor she would probably never have become a star.

'Did she get on with Louis?' I asked, my lips so close to her cheek that I could feel the warmth of my own breath come back to me.

'I don't think he ever let her get away with anything. He's just as vain as she was only in a nice way. Everybody likes Louis. He pads, you know.'

'He what?'

'You know . . . like a falsie: well, they say he wears one, too, when he's in tights.'

'Oh, no, he doesn't,' I said, remembering my little tussle with the ballet's glamour boy.

'You too?' She sat bolt upright.

'Me too what?'

'He didn't . . . go after you, too, did he?'

'Well, as a matter of fact he did but I fought him off.' And I told her the story of how I had saved my honor.

She was very sceptical. 'He's had every boy in the company . . . even the ones who like girls . . . I expect he's irresistible.'

'I resisted.'

'Well . . .' And then it began.

5

'Jane.' There was no answer. Light streamed into the room but she wore a black mask over her eyes, and nothing else . . . the sheets lay tangled in a heap upon the floor beside the bed. It was another hot day I could tell. Yawning, I sat up and looked at my watch which I had placed on the night table; I've always taken it off, ever since a girl from Vassar complained that it scratched. Ten-thirty.

I lit a cigarette and studied the body sprawled next to me in a position which, in any other woman, would have been unattractive. In her case, however, she could be suspended from a chandelier and she would look good enough to take home right then and there.

I leaned over and tickled her smooth belly, like pink alabaster, to become lyric, warm pink alabaster, gently curved, with hips strong and fatless and lovely breasts tilted neither up nor down nor sagging, but properly centered, the work of a first-rate architect: not one of those slapdash jobs you come across so often in this life. She sighed and moved away, not yet awake. I then tickled the breast nearest me and she said, very clearly, 'You cut that out.'

'That's not a very romantic way to begin the morning,' I said. She pulled off her mask and scowled in the sunlight which streamed into the high-ceilinged dusty room. Then she smiled when she saw me. 'I forgot,' she said. She stretched.

'I'm scared to look at the papers,' I said.

She groaned. 'And I thought it was going to be such a perfect day. It's so hot,' she added irrelevantly, sitting up. I admired her nonchalance. She was the first girl I had ever known who had been agreeable and affectionate without ever once speaking of love. I decided that I was going to like ballet very much.

'I have a headache,' she announced, blinking her eyes and pressing her temples with her hands.

'I got just the cure for it,' I said, rolling toward her.

She took one look and said, 'Not now. It's too hot.' But her voice lacked conviction and our bodies met as we repeated with even greater intensity the act of the night before, our breath coming in short gasps until, at the climax, there was no one else in the whole world but the two of us on that bed, the sunlight streaming in the window and the springs creaking, our bodies making funny wet noises as the bellies pushed one against the other.

When it was over, Jane went into the bathroom and I lay

with my eyes shut, the sweat drying on my body, as blissfully relaxed as that young man in the painting by Michelangelo. But then, in the midst of this euphoria, I decided that I should call Mr. Washburn and get my orders for the day. It was early of course for our business and, in ordinary times, no one would be stirring at this hour during the season but today with a murder on our hand . . . a murder. . . . It wasn't until that moment, lying contented and exhausted on a strange girl's bed, that I realized the significance of what had happened, of what the sudden death of Ella Sutton might mean to all of us, including me, the newcomer, the fool who had found a pair of shears and . . .

I got Mr. Washburn on the line. 'Been trying to locate you,' he said and I could tell from his voice that he was worried. 'Get over to the Met at eleven, will you? The police are going to talk to us, to the principals.'

'I'll be there, sir.'

'Did you see the papers this morning?'

'Quite something, weren't they?' I said, implying I had read them which I had not.

'Made the front page . . . even of the *Times*,' said my employer in a voice which sounded almost joyous. 'We'll have to change our strategy . . . but I'll go into all that when I see you.'

I then called Miss Flynn at my own office.

'I tried to reach you at your home, Mr. Sargeant, *but there was no answer*.' Miss Flynn is the only human being I have ever known who could talk not only in itals but, on occasion, could make her silences sound as meaningful as asterisks.

'I was busy all night . . . working,' I said lamely.

'I hope you will try and get some rest today, Mr. Sargeant.'

'I hope so, too. But you know what happened . . .'

'Yes, I saw some mention of it in the *Times*. One of those dancers was murdered.'

'Yes, and we're all being questioned. It's going to be quite a public relations job.'

' *   *   *   *   *   *   * '

'I probably won't get to the office today . . . so refer any call to me at the office of the ballet.'

'Yes, Mr. Sargeant.'

I then gave her some instructions about the night school, the hat company and the television actress who had just been voted Miss Tangerine of Central California by an old buddy of mine who lived out there and was a member of the Chamber of Commerce of Marysville.

Jane was dressed by the time I had finished . . . like all girls connected with the theater she could be a quick changer if she wanted. I told her that I had to join Washburn and the principals at the opera house. While I dressed it was agreed that we meet after tonight's performance and come directly here . . . presuming, of course, that there would be a performance. I had no idea of what the police attitude would be.

'I'll go take class now,' she said, pinning her hair up. 'Then I suppose I should go and see poor Magda.'

'Magda who?' I had forgotten.

'The girl who fainted last night. She's a good friend of mine.'

'The one who was pregnant?'

'How did you know?'

'Everybody knows,' I said, as though I had been in ballet all my life. But then curiosity got the better of me. 'Who was the father?'

Jane smiled. 'I thought you would have found that out, too. *Everybody* knows.'

'They forgot to tell me.'

'Miles Sutton is the lucky man,' said Jane, but she wasn't smiling now and I could see why.

II

I DON'T know when I'd seen so many gloomy faces as I did that morning in Eglanova's dressing rooms. Mr. Gleason of the Police Department had assembled the company's brass there, with the exception of Eglanova herself and Louis, neither of whom had yet arrived. But the others were there . . . including Miles Sutton who looked as though he hadn't slept in a week, his eyes glassy with fatigue, and Jed Wilbur who kept cracking his knuckles until I thought I'd go crazy and Mr. Washburn in a handsome summer suit, very grave, and Alyosha looking fairly relaxed, as well as the stage manager and a few other notables who stood about the room while Detective Gleason, a round pig of a man with a cigar, obligingly revealed to us the full splendor of the official mind.

'Where are those two dancers . . . Egg-something and Giraffe?'

Egg and Giraffe . . . pretty good, I thought, giving him an A for effort.

'They will be along shortly,' said Mr. Washburn soothingly. 'After all, this is very early for them to be up.'

'Early!' snorted Gleason. 'That's a funny way to run a business.'

'It is an art, not a business,' said Alyosha mildly.

Gleason looked at him suspiciously. 'What is your name again?'

'Alyosha Petrovich Rudin.'

'A Russian, eh?'

'Originally.'

The detective scowled a xenophobe's scowl but made no comment. He had us where he wanted us but then again we were pretty hot stuff, too, and we had *him* if he got too frisky. I was quite sure that Mr. Washburn was in hourly contact with City Hall.

'Well, we'll start without them. First, I think you should all know that there's been a murder.' He consulted a piece of paper which he held in his hand. 'Ella Sutton was murdered last night at ten-thirty, by falling. The cable which was holding her thirty-eight feet above the stage was severed, except for one strand, by a party or parties as yet unknown, between the hours of four-thirty and ten p.m. . . . We have, by the way, what we believe to be the murder weapon: a pair of shears which are now being tested for fingerprints and also for metal filings, to see if they correspond with the metal of the cable.' He paused and fixed us with a steely eye, as though expecting the murderer to burst into hysterical sobs and confess everything; instead it was I who almost burst into hysterical sobs, thinking of those damned shears and how I had handled them. I had several very bad minutes.

'Now, I'll be frank with you,' said Gleason, who was obviously going to be no such thing, now or ever. 'We could close down your show while we investigate but, for one reason and another, we've decided to let you finish up your last two weeks here, just as you planned, and we'll investigate when we can. Believe me when I say it's a real break for you.' I looked at Mr. Washburn, the intimate of Kings and Mayors, but he was looking very bland indeed. 'I want to warn you folks, though, that none of you is to take French leave, to disappear from the scene of the crime during your last week, or later, if we haven't wound this case up by then . . . and I think we will have, by then,' he added ominously, looking, I swear, right at me, as though he'd already found my fingerprints on what was now called The Murder Weapon. I felt faint. Love and a possible accusation of being a murderer need a full stomach, coffee anyway.

'To be frank with you,' said Gleason, obviously bent on being a good fellow, 'it seems very likely that the murder was committed by someone closely connected with the theater, by someone who knew all about the new ballet and who had a grudge against Miss Sutton. . . .' Bravo, I said to myself. You are cooking with gas, Gleason. I began to insult him in my mind . . . for some reason I was perfectly willing to let the murderer go undetected. Sutton was no great loss but then, of course, I am callous, having been an infantryman at Okinawa (wounded my first day of action, by a bullet in the left buttock . . . no, I was *not* running away; the bullet ricocheted, I swear to God, and I was carried from the field, all bloody from my baptism of fire).

'I will,' said Mr. Gleason, 'interview each and every one of you, starting right now and continuing through the entire company, including the stagehands . . . every one, in short, who was backstage.' He unfolded a long sheet of paper, a list of names. 'Here is the list in the order in which I want to see you people. Will you have it put some place where the other members of the company can see it?' Mr. Washburn said that he would and motioned for the stage manager to take it outside and put it on the bulletin board.

When the stage manager returned, he was accompanied by Eglanova and Louis. Eglanova looked very distinguished in a black lace dress of mourning with a white feathered hat on her head, while Louis wore a pair of slacks and a sport shirt like the *Tennis Anyone?* juvenile he occasionally resembles.

'So sorry,' said Eglanova, swooping down upon the Inspector. 'You are the police? I am Madame Eglanova . . . this is *my* dressing room,' she added, intimating that we had all better get the hell out of there.

'Pleased to meet you,' said Gleason, obviously impressed.

'And I am Louis Giraud,' said Louis with great dignity, but it didn't come off because Gleason was too busy explaining things to Eglanova who was carefully maneuvering him to the door, like a stalking lioness. In a few minutes we were all out of there and Gleason repaired to an office on the second floor to commence his interviews . . . the first, naturally enough, was Miles Sutton. I was number seven on the list, I noticed. Lucky seven?

I cornered Mr. Washburn outside in the street; we both had gone out, automatically, for the afternoon papers. 'I've got something to tell you,' I said.

'I want to hear only good news,' said Mr. Washburn warningly. 'I have had enough disaster to last me the rest of what, very likely, will be a short life. My heart is not strong.'

'I'm sorry to hear that, sir, but I think you should know something about those shears.'

'Those what?'

'The things the police thought the murderer cut the cable with.'

'Well, what about them?'

'It just so happens that I found them last night in the wastebasket in Eglanova's room.'

'What were they doing there?' Mr. Washburn was deep in *The Journal-American* . . . we were still on the front page.

'Somebody put them there.'

'Very likely . . . I wonder why they always spell Eglanova's name wrong? According to this account, it's all a Communist plot.'

'Mr. Washburn, *I* moved those shears . . . I picked them up and I took them out of that dressing room and put them on top of the toolbox backstage.'

'Very tidy. You'd be surprised at the size of our bill for tools every month . . . especially things getting lost. By the way, the box office reported that we're sold out until closing night. You better get *that* in the papers tomorrow.'

'Yes sir, but I . . .'

'You know this may not be such a bad thing . . . I mean, of course, it's perfectly awful and God knows where I'm ever going to get a ballerina for next season . . . but it's certainly put *Eclipse* on the map. Everybody will want to see it from here to San Francisco, a real draw.' At this moment, I found Mr. Washburn a trifle materialistic, even for an old-fashioned opportunist like me.

'Maybe Eglanova will go with the company again next year,' I suggested, forgetting my own peril for a brief moment.

'But she wants to retire and we should let her,' said Mr. Washburn, starting in on *The World-Telegram and Sun*; he made Eglanova's retirement sound like her choice rather than his.

'I heard Markova is tied up with her new company.'

'True . . . she's too expensive anyway.'

'And so are Toumanova, Alonso, Danilova and Tallchief,' said I, repeating what Jane had told me the night before.

'Editorial in the *Telegram*,' said Mr. Washburn gravely. 'They want to know if Wilbur is a Communist.'

'I had forgotten all about that,' I said truthfully.

'Well, I haven't. The Veterans Committee telephoned to say that their pickets would be back tonight and that they would have new placards, calling us the Murder Company as well as the Red Company.'

'That's a laugh!'

'I am not sure on whom, though,' said Mr. Washburn, studying the *Post* which had by far the best and sexiest pictures of Sutton, and no mention of the Red menace.

'Is Wilbur worried?'

31

'He seems to be. I'm supposed to have a talk with him this afternoon. Well, that's that,' he said, handing the papers to me.

Outside the stage door a policeman in plain-clothes lounged; he looked at us suspiciously as we entered.

'An armed camp!' exclaimed my employer with more gusto than I for one thought proper under the circumstances; our roles were reversed now: I was the one bothered by the publicity and investigation while he was the one who was meditating happily on free promotion and the coming tour with the customers flocking to see the 'murder' ballet.

'By the way,' I said, 'who's going to dance the lead in *Eclipse* tonight . . . you have it scheduled, you know, and I should get a release out for the morning papers.'

'Good God! Where's Wilbur?' The stage manager, hearing this, went to find the beleaguered choreographer.

'How would this Jane Garden do? I'm told she's very fine.' I said, getting in a plug for the home team.

'It's up to him . . . after all we've got three soloists.'

'I think she'd be great in it.' Then, changing from my youthful, eager manner to that somewhat more austere manner which is more nearly me, I said, 'About those shears that I found in Eglanova's room.'

'What about them?' We went through the whole thing again and, for the second time in five minutes, he was upset.

'What I want to know is should I tell the police right now that I found the shears in her room and put them outside on the tool chest, or should I wait until the Inspector arrests me for murder, after finding my prints all over The Murder Weapon.'

Mr. Washburn looked exactly like a man being goosed by the cold horns of the biggest, roughest dilemma this side of the Bronx Zoo. Needless to say, between sacrificing his star and his temporary Press agent, he chose yours truly, as I suspected he would, to be offered up as a possible sacrifice to Miss Justice, that blind girl with the sword. 'You can do something for me, Peter,' he said, in the cozy voice of an impresario talking to a millionaire.

'Anything, sir,' I said, very sincerely, looking at him with honest cocker spaniel eyes . . . little did he suspect that I was contemplating blackmail, that my mean little mind had seized upon a brilliant idea which would, if it worked, make me very

32

happy indeed and if it didn't . . . well, I could always take a lie-detector test or something to prove that I hadn't eased Ella Sutton into a better and lovelier world.

'Say nothing about this, Son. Not until the season is over . . . just a week away. That's all I ask. I'm sure they won't go after you . . . absolutely sure. You have no motive. You didn't even know Sutton. On top of that . . . well, I have a little influence in this town, as you know. Believe me when I say there won't be any trouble.'

'If you say so, Mr. Washburn, then I won't tell the police.' I then asked that Jane Garden be given the lead in *Eclipse* (she was understudy anyway), and she got it. Perfidy had paid off.

'I suppose she'll be all right,' said Wilbur a few minutes later when he'd been advised of this casting. 'She's up in the part at least. I'd much rather have a dark-haired girl, but . . .'

'Garden should be very good,' said Mr. Washburn. 'You'd better rehearse her and Louis this afternoon.'

'I'll go telephone her,' I said, and I did. At first, she didn't believe it but then, when she did, she was beside herself and I knew we were going to have a pleasant time . . . champagne in bed, I decided, as I hung up.

My second official interview with the Inspector went off well enough.

'How old are you?'

'Twenty-eight.'

'Where were you born?'

'Hartford, Connecticut.'

'In the service?'

'Three and a half years . . . Pacific Theater of Operations . . . Army.'

'What sort of work did you do upon discharge?'

'Went back to college . . . finished at Harvard.'

'Harvard?'

'Yes, *Harvard*.' We glared at one another.

'What sort of work after that?'

'I was assistant drama critic on the *Globe* until a year ago when I opened my own office . . . public relations.'

'I see. How long have you known, did you know, the deceased?'

'Who?'

'Miss Sutton . . . who did you think I meant? Mayor La Guardia?'

'I'm sorry if I misunderstood you, Mr. Gleason.' Oh, I was in splendid form, putting my head right into the noose, but what the hell . . . tonight there'd be champagne. 'I met Miss Sutton the day I came to work for the ballet . . . yesterday afternoon.'

'As what?'

'As special public relations consultant . . . that's what it says on that paper in front of you.'

'Are you trying to get funny with me?'

'Certainly not.' I looked offended.

'How well did you know the . . . Miss Sutton?'

'I met her yesterday.'

'You never saw her outside of work then?'

'Not very often.'

'How often?'

'Never, then.'

'Well, which is it, never or occasionally?'

'Never, I guess, to speak of . . . maybe now and then at a party before I'd met her . . . that's all I meant.'

'It would help if you say what you mean the first time.'

'I'll try.'

'Did she have any enemies that you know of?'

'Well, yes and no.'

'Yes *or* no, please, Mr. Sargeant.'

'No . . . not that I know of. On the other hand, I gather that nobody liked her.'

'And why was that?'

'I'm told she wasn't very easy to work with and she was unpleasant to the kids in the company, especially the girls. She was set to be the big star when Eglanova retired.'

'I see. Does Egg . . . lanova look forward to retiring?'

'Wouldn't you after thirty years in ballet?'

'I'm not in ballet.'

'Well, neither am I, Mr. Gleason. I know almost as little about this as you.'

Gleason gave me an extremely dirty look but I was full of beans, thinking about how I had handled Washburn.

'Was her marriage to Miles Sutton a happy one?'

'I suggest you ask him; I've never met him.'

'I see.' Gleason was getting a little red in the face and I could

34

see that I was amusing his secretary, a pale youth who was taking down our conversation in shorthand.

'Now then: where were you at the dress rehearsal yesterday afternoon?'

'Backstage mostly.'

'Did you notice anything unusual?'

'Like what?'

'Like . . . never mind. What were your movements *after* the rehearsal?'

'Well, I went out and had a sandwich; then I called up the different newspapers . . . about the Wilbur business. I got back to the theater about five-thirty.'

'And you left it?'

'Not until after the murder last night.'

'Who did you see when you returned at five-thirty, who was backstage?'

'Just about everyone, I suppose: Mr. Washburn, Eglanova, Giraud, Rudin . . . no, he wasn't there until about six, and neither was Miles Sutton now that I think of it.'

'Is it customary for all these people to be in the theater such a long time before a performance?'

'I don't know . . . it was a première night.'

'Eglanova was not in the première, though, was she?'

'No, but she often spends the day in the theater . . . so does Giraud. He sleeps.'

'By the way, do you happen to know who will take Sutton's place tonight?'

I paused just long enough to sound guilty; I kicked myself but there was nothing to be done about it. 'Jane Garden . . . one of the younger soloists.'

But he missed the connection, I could see, and not until all the interviews had been neatly typed up and my fingerprints had been discovered on the shears would he decide that I had cut the cable so that Jane could dance the lead in *Eclipse.*

He asked me a few more questions to which I gave some mighty flip answers and then he told me to go, very glad to see the last of me, for that day at least. I have a dislike of policemen which must be the real thing since I'd never had anything to do with them up until now, outside of the traffic cops. There is something about the state putting the power to bully into the hands of a group of subnormal, sadistic apes that makes my blood boil. Of course, the good citizens would say that it takes an ape to keep the other apes in line but then again it is piteous indeed to listen to the yowls of those same good citizens when they come afoul the law and are beaten up in prisons and generally man-handled for suspected or for real crimes: at such moments they probably wish they had done something about the guardians of law and order when they were free. Well, it was no problem of mine at the moment.

I found Jane already downstairs in her rehearsal clothes. I gave her a big kiss and then, when she asked me if I had had any-thing to do with her getting the lead in *Eclipse* and I said that I certainly had, I got another kiss. She asked me all about the investigation.

'Everybody's being pumped,' I said. 'They just got through with me. You better go look on the bulletin board and find out what time they'll want to see you.' We looked; and she was to be questioned at six o'clock.

'What did he want to know?'

'Just stuff. Where I was when it happened . . . who else was around, and gossip.'

'What did you tell him?'

'Not much of anything . . . in the way of gossip; it's his job to find out those things.'

'I suppose it is.'

Wilbur and Louis appeared, both in work clothes. 'Come on, Jane,' said Louis. 'We got work.' He winked at me. 'How're you doing, Baby?'

I called him a rude but accurate name and marched off to telephone the newspapers about Jane's coming debut as a soloist . . . it wouldn't get in till tomorrow but then, perhaps, we might be able to get a few of the critics out to report on her the next night. Needless to say, we were scheduled to do *Eclipse* at every single performance until we closed. After I had made my calls and arranged for some photographs of Jane to be sent around by messenger, I left the building with every intention of going to get something to eat . . . I was getting light in the head from hunger and the heat. I was so giddy that I almost stepped on Miles Sutton who was lying face down in the corridor which leads from the office to the dressing rooms.

'What's going on here?' were, I am ashamed to say, my first words to what I immediately, and inaccurately, thought to be a corpse, the discarded earthly residence of our conductor who lay spread-eagled on his belly in front of the washroom door.

The figure at my feet moaned softly and, thinking of finger-prints, I nevertheless was a good Samaritan and rolled him over on his back, half expecting to see the hilt of a quaint oriental dagger sticking through his coat.

'Water,' whispered Miles Sutton, and I got him water from the bathroom; he drank it very sloppily and then, rolling up his eyes the way certain comedians do when their material is weak, he sank back on to the floor, very white in the face. I trotted back into the bathroom, got another cup of water, returned, and splashed it in his face. This had the desired effect. He opened his eyes and sat up. 'Must've fainted,' he whispered in a weak voice.

'So it would appear,' I said; at the moment there was very little the conductor and I had in common. I stood there for several seconds, contemplating him; then Sutton pulled out a handkerchief and dried his beard. His color was a little better now and I suggested that, all in all, it might be a good idea for him to stand up. I helped him to his feet. He lurched into the washroom; I waited until he came out.

'Must be the heat,' he mumbled. 'Sort of thing never happened before.'

'It's a hot day,' I said . . . it was remarkable how little we had to say to each other. 'Do you feel O.K. now?'

'A bit shaky.'

I don't feel so good myself,' I said, hunger gnawing at my vitals. 'Why don't we get something to eat across the street? I'm Peter Sargeant, by the way: I'm handling publicity. I don't think Mr. Washburn introduced us.'

We shook hands; then he said, dubiously, 'I don't suppose I should hang around here. They may want me for the rehearsal.'

'Come on,' I said, and he did. Very slowly we walked down the brilliant sunlit street; shimmering waves of heat flickered in the distance and my shirt began to stick to my back. Miles, looking as though he might faint again, breathed hoarsely, like an old dog having a nightmare.

'Must have been something you ate?' I suggested out of my vast reservoir of small talk.

He looked rather bleak and didn't answer as we walked into an air-conditioned restaurant with plywood walls got up to look like the paneling in an old English tavern; both of us perked up considerably.

'Or maybe you got hold of a bad piece of ice last night.' This was unworthy of me but I didn't care. I was thinking of food.

We got ourselves a booth and neither of us spoke until I had wolfed down a large breakfast and he had had several cups of coffee. By this time he was looking less like a corpse. I knew very little about him other than that he got good notices for himself and orchestra, that he conducted the important ballets with more than usual attention to the often eclectic performances of the Grand Saint Petersburg stars who have a tendency to impose their own tempo on that of the dead and defenseless composers. I disliked his face, but that means nothing at all. My character analyses based on physiognomy or intuition are, without exception, incorrect; even so I have many profound likes and dislikes based entirely on the set of a man's eyes or his voice. I did not like Sutton's eyes, I might add, large grey glassy eyes with immense black pupils, and an expression of constant surprise. He fixed me now with these startled eyes and said, 'Did you talk to the Inspector?'

'Just for a little bit.'

'What did he ask you?'

'Nothing much . . . the standard questions . . . where were you on the night of May twenty-seventh kind of thing.'

'Such an awful thing to have happened,' said the husband of the murdered woman with startling conventionality; well, at least he wasn't hypocrite enough to pretend to be griefstricken. 'I suppose everybody's told him we weren't getting along, Ella and me.'

'I didn't,' I said, righteously, 'but obviously he knows. He wanted me to say that you hated her . . . I could tell by his questions.'

'He practically accused me of murder,' said Miles; I felt very sorry for him then not only because of the spot he was in but because I was quite sure that he *had* murdered her . . . which shows something or other about mid-twentieth-century morality: I mean, we seem to be less and less aroused by such things as

38

private murders in an age when public murder is so much admired. If I ever get around to writing that novel it's going to be about this sort of thing . . . the difference between what we say and what we do—you know what I mean. Anyway, *I* didn't make the world.

'Well, you are a perfect setup,' I said, cold-bloodedly.

'Setup?'

'Everybody in the company knew you wanted a divorce and that she wouldn't give it to you . . . I heard all about it my first hour with the company.'

'That doesn't mean I'd kill her.'

'No, but a cretin like Gleason would think that you are the logical one . . . and you are.'

'I'm not so sure of that.'

'What do you mean?'

'Well, there are others.' He looked purposefully vague and I felt very compassionate; he *was* in a spot.

'Who?'

'Well, there's Eglanova.' That did it; my instinct was right. Miles had cut the cable and then planted the shears in Eglanova's wastebasket. I wondered if he had managed to implicate her in his interview with Gleason.

'What did she have against Sutton?' Not that I didn't know.

'She was being retired against her will and Ella was the only available dancer with a big enough name to head the company. . . . All the others are either tied up with contracts or else cost more than Washburn will pay. With Ella gone, he would have to let Eglanova dance another season.'

'It seems awfully tragic,' I said mildly.

'You don't know much about ballerinas,' said Miles Sutton with the exhausted air of one who did. 'Eglanova doesn't want to retire, ever; she feels she's at her peak and she would do anything to stay with the company.'

'But that's still going a bit far.'

'She hated Ella.'

'So did just about everybody; they didn't all kill her . . . or maybe they did . . . formed a committee and . . .' But, no, this was getting a little too feckless, even for me. I subsided.

'Besides, who else could have done it? Who else would benefit as much by her death?' Well, you would, lover, I said to myself, you you you, wonderful you in the shadow of the electric chair.

He must've read my mind, which isn't as difficult a feat as I sometimes like to think. 'Aside from me,' he added.

'So far as we know.'

'So far as *I* know, and I should know . . . I was married to her seven years.'

'Why wouldn't she let you have a divorce?'

He shrugged, 'I don't know. She was like that . . . a real sadist. She married me when she was just a *corps de ballet* girl and of course I helped her up the ladder. I suppose she resented that. People usually resent the ones who help them.'

'Why didn't you just go ahead and divorce her?'

'Too complicated,' said Miles, evasively, looking away, tugging at his wiry orange beard. 'By the way, will you be at the inquest tomorrow?'

I said no, that this was the first I'd heard of it.

'I have to be there,' said Miles gloomily. 'The funeral's after that.'

'Church funeral?' I made a mental note to call the photographers.

'No, just a chapel in a funeral home. I got her a lot out at Woodlawn.'

'Very expensive?'

'What? No, not very . . . the funeral home handled everything. Awfully efficient crowd.'

'It's a big racket,' I said.

'I know, but it saves all sorts of trouble.'

'Open or closed casket at the service?'

'Closed. You see there was an autopsy this morning.'

'What did they find?'

'I don't know. Gleason didn't say. Probably nothing.'

'You know,' I said, suddenly struck by a novel idea, 'it might have been an accident after all.'

Miles Sutton groaned. 'If only it were! No, I'm afraid they've already proved that those shears did the trick. Gleason told me that the metal filings corresponded to the metal of the cable.'

A cold chill went up my spine, and it wasn't the Polar Bear Airconditioning Unit for Theaters, Restaurants and Other Public Places. 'What about fingerprints?'

'They didn't say.'

'Fingerprints are pretty old-fashioned now, anyway,' I

40

brazened. 'Every kid knows enough not to leave them around where the police might find them.'

'Then Jed Wilbur could have done it,' mused Sutton. 'He never got along with Ella.'

'But, as I keep pointing out, even in a ballet company dislike is insufficient motive for murder.'

'Maybe he had a motive,' said Miles mysteriously, kicking up some more dust. I'll say this for him, if Miles did his act with the police the way he did with me he'd keep them busy for a year untangling the politics and private relationships of the Grand Saint Petersburg Ballet.

'Well, motive or not, he's not the kind of person to endanger his career. That gentleman is the opportunist of all times. If he was going to knock off a dancer he wouldn't do it on the opening night of his greatest masterpiece . . .'

'Even so,' said Miles, reminding me of the giant squid in those underwater movies . . . spreading black ink like a smoke screen at the first sign of danger. 'And what about Alyosha Rudin?'

'What about him?'

'Didn't you know?'

'Know? Know what?'

'He was Ella's lover before she met me. He got her into ballet when she was just another chorine.'

'Well, I'll be damned.' This was a bit of gossip I hadn't heard.

'He's been in love with her all these years . . . even after she married me.'

'Why would she marry you to get ahead when she had the *regisseur* of the company in love with her?'

Miles chuckled. 'He wouldn't help her . . . thought she couldn't dance classical roles worth a damn . . . which was quite true, then. She was just another little girl who hadn't studied enough. But he didn't take into account her ambition, which I did. I got her solos in spite of him and she was always good. She was one of those people who could do anything you gave her to do well, even though you might have thought she'd fall flat on her face.'

'And Alyosha?'

'He was surprised how well she turned out.'

'And he stayed in love with her?'

'So she always said.'

'He seems a little old for that kind of thing.'

41

Miles grunted to show that I was too young to know the facts of age. Then we paid our checks and went back to the theater. A crowd of newsmen met us at the door. Miles scooted inside quickly and I paused to butter them up a little, promising them impossible interviews in my dishonest press-agent way; they were on to my game but we had a pleasant time and I *was* able to tell them about the funeral the next day; I promised them full details later, time and place and so on.

I watched the end of the rehearsal. I knew that, as a rule, rehearsals which involve just the principals don't take place on the stage but at the West Side Studio; in this case, however, Wilbur had insisted on rehearsing Louis and Jane on stage to the music of one piano. He wanted to get Jane used to the stage, immediately.

She looked very efficient, I thought, as I sat on the first row and watched her move through the intricate *pas de deux* with Louis; she acted as though she had been dancing leads all her life and I experienced a kind of parental pride. Wilbur seemed pleased; especially with the way she did her turns fifteen feet above the stage, scaring the life out of me as I recalled the night before . . . it was just possible that we had some homicidal maniac in the company who enjoyed seeing ballerinas take fatal pratfalls. If Jane was at all aware of any danger she certainly didn't show it, as she pretended to eclipse the sun with a transfigured expression that I had seen on her face only once before, that morning when she had slid blissfully into a hot bath.

'All right, kids, that's enough for today. You'll be fine, Jane,' said Jed Wilbur as she came floating down out of the ceiling. 'Remember to take it a little slower in your solo. Keep it muted, lyric. Remember what you're doing . . . when in doubt go slow. The music will hold you up. You have a tendency to be too sharp in your line, too classical . . . blur it a little.' And the three walked off stage. I headed for the office where we had the largest stack of mail I think I have ever seen . . . requests for tickets, for souvenir fragments of the cable, as well as advice from ballet lovers on how to conduct the investigation; I'll say one thing for the balletomanes, they really know their stuff; they follow the lives and careers of their favorites with rapt attention and remarkable shrewdness. Many of the letters that I glanced at openly suggested that Miles Sutton and his late wife had not been on the

best of terms . . . now how could strangers have known that?
From the columnists?

Mr. Washburn summoned me into the inner office, a spacious room with a thick carpet and a number of Cecil Beaton photographs of our stars, past and present, on the walls. He looked fit, I thought, in spite of the heat and excitement.

'The police have been very agreeable,' he chuckled, handing me one of those special filtered cigarettes which I particularly dislike. I took it anyway. 'They have consented not only to let us finish our season but, after the inquest tomorrow, to conduct the investigation a little more discreetly than had been Gleason's intention.' Mr. Washburn looked like a very satisfied shark at that moment . . . one who had been swimming about all day in the troubled waters of City Hall. 'There'll be two plainclothes men backstage at every performance and, of course, no member of the company is allowed to leave New York . . . *and* they all must be available at a moment's notice, leave messages where they can be found.'

'What's our policy about the funeral tomorrow afternoon?' I asked, after I had first assured my employer that his wishes were, as always, my command.

Mr. Washburn frowned. 'I suppose the principals had better attend. I'll be there of course . . . you, too.'

'And the Press?'

He gave me a lecture on the dignity of death, the privacy of sorrow; after which he agreed that the Press should be fully represented at the last rites.

Then I asked if I should give Jane the full star treatment and he said we should first wait and see what the reviewers would have to say about her . . . needless to say they were all turning up again tonight. After that, he gave me some routine orders, ending with the announcement that Anna Eglanova would tour another year with the company, her thirty-second year as a star.

'When did you sign her?'

'This afternoon. She changed her mind about retiring, as I knew she would.' He was very smooth.

Neither of us made any mention of the murder. Mr. Washburn had taken the public line that it had all been an accident, that no one connected with his company could have done such a thing but that of course if the police wanted to investigate, well, that was their right. In private he also maintained this pose and for all

43

I knew he really believed it. In any case, his main interest was the box office and that had never been so healthy since Nijinski danced a season with the company a long time ago. If someone had the bad taste to murder a fellow artist he would wash his hands of them.

3

I was almost sick to my stomach during that night's performance . . . experiencing double stage fright for Jane: first, because it was her big chance, as they say in technicolor movies, and second, because of that cable.

Everyone in the audience was also keyed up. They looked like a group of wolves waiting for dinner. There was absolute silence all through the ballet . . . even when Louis, who is after all a big star, came on stage with that pearly smile which usually gets all the girls and gay boys.

Jane was better than I thought she would be. I don't know why but you never regard your lover as being remarkably talented; you never seem to think her able to do anything at all unusual or brilliant unless, of course, she's a big star or very well known when you first meet her, in which case, you soon discover that she's not at all what she's cracked up to be . . . but Jane floored me and, I am happy to say, the critics, too. She lost the music once or twice and there was a terrible moment when Louis fumbled a lift, when she sprang too soon and I thought they would land in a heap on the stage but both recovered like real professionals and by the time she began her ascent by cable I knew that she was in, really there at last.

I don't need to tell you that I watched her rise in the air, slowly turning, with my heart thudding crazily and all my pulses fluttering. Even when the curtain fell I half expected to hear a crash from backstage. But it was all right and there she was, a moment later, standing on the stage with Louis, the *corps de ballet* behind them, as the audience roared its excitement, relief, disappointment . . . everything, every emotion swept over that stage like surf on a beach. She took seven curtain calls, by herself, and received all four of my bouquets as well as two others, from strangers.

I ran backstage and found her in Sutton's dressing room (now

44

hers) with most of the company congratulating her, out of relief as well as admiration. I think they were all afraid that something might happen again. . . .

Then the stage manager ordered everybody to get upstairs and change and I was left alone with Jane in the dressing room, among the flowers and telegrams from those friends who had been alerted.

'I'm glad it's over,' she said at last, her eyes gleaming, still breathing hard.

'So am I. I was terrified.'

'Me too.'

'Of that cable?'

'No, just the part. I didn't have time to think of anything else. You have no idea what it's like to come out on a stage and know that every eye is on you.'

'It must be wonderful.'

'It is! It is!' She slipped out of her costume and I dried her off with a towel . . . her skin glowed, warm and rich, like silk. I kissed her, here and there.

4

There is no need to describe my evening with Jane. It was a memorable one for both of us and, next morning, the sun seemed intolerably bright as we awakened, showered, got dressed, ate breakfast . . . all in a terrible hung-over silence which did not end until, of mutual accord, still without a word, we each took an Empirin tablet and together threw out the three empty champagne bottles (Mumm, Rheims, France); then I spoke: ' "April," ' I said thickly, ' "is the cruelest month." '

'This is May,' said Jane.

'And twice as cruel. I have a strange feeling that during the night the spores of some mysterious fungus or moss, wafted down from the planet Venus, lodged themselves in my brain, entering through some unguarded orifice. Everything is fuzzy and blurred and I don't hear so well.'

'You sound like you're still lit,' said Jane, putting on a pink negligee which she had once bought at a sale to make herself look seductive over the morning coffee. Wearing only jockey

45

shorts, I posed like Atlas before the full-length mirror on the bathroom door.

'Do you think I'd make a dancer?'

'You've made me, darling,' she said.

'Shall I wash your mouth out with soap?'

'I'm sorry. It won't happen again.'

'Not even on alternate Wednesdays?'

'That's matinee day . . . when I do *Eclipse*, twice.' And that was the end of our little game. In case you should ever have an affair with a dancer I recommend total resignation to the fact that the Dance comes first; not only in their lives (which is all right) but also in *your* life (which is not, unless you're a dancer, too, or connected with it the way I am). After a time you will gradually forget all about the other world of Republicans and Democrats, Communists and Capitalists, Hemingway, the D. and D. of Windsor and Leo Durocher. I suppose in a way it's kind of a refuge from the world, like a monastery or a nudist colony . . . except for the tourists: the lives of dancers are filled with the comings and goings of little friends and admirers, autograph hounds and lovers, and you never know who is likely to turn up backstage in hot pursuit of one of the girls, or boys. I've been very surprised, believe me, at certain respectable gentlemen who have unexpectedly revealed a Socratic passion for one of our dancing boys. If I should ever decide to go into the blackmail game I could certainly get some handsome retainers!

Midway through an analysis of her last night's performance in *Eclipse*, the phone began to ring: friends and relatives of the new star . . . so I left her to enjoy their admiration.

It was another hot day, windless and still, with not a cloud in the harsh blue sky. I walked to our office, keeping in the shade of buildings, enjoying the occasional blasts of icy air from the open doors of restaurants and bars.

The newspapers were very gratifying. We were still on the front page, or near it, and the *Globe* had a feature article on the life of Ella Sutton, implying, as did nearly all the other papers, that an arrest would soon be made, that the murderer was her husband . . . naturally, they all kept this side of libel; even so it was perfectly clear that they thought him guilty . . . all except the *Mirror* which thought it was a Communist plot. The *Globe* carried a six-column story of Ella's life with pictures of her from every phase of what turned out to be a longer and more varied career than even I had suspected. Dancers are such liars (and so are Press agents, God knows) that as a result the facts of any star's life are so obscure that it would take a real detective to discover them, or else a good reporter with access to a first-rate morgue, like the *Globe's*.

There was nobody in the office; except one secretary, another sack of mail, and so many messages marked urgent that I didn't bother to look at any of them; instead, I just relaxed and read the true story of Ella's life. I was surprised to note that she was thirty-three years old when she crossed the shining river so abruptly, that she had been dancing professionally for twenty years, in burlesque, in second-rate musical comedies and, finally, in the celebrated but short-lived North American Ballet Company which was to ballet in the thirties what the Group Theater was to the drama . . . only a good deal more left wing than the Group, if possible. There was a photograph of her at that time all done up like a Russian peasant woman with her eyes looking north to the stars. When the North American folded, she danced for a time in night clubs; then, just before the war, Demidovna emerged on our startled ken, to be rechristened the next year Ella Sutton, prima ballerina but never *assoluta*. It was a good piece and I made a mental note to call the *Globe* and find out who had written it . . . the by-line Milton Haddock meant nothing, I knew.

The next few hours were occupied with business . . . the ballet's and my own. Miss Flynn implied that my presence in my office might make a good impression. I promised to drop by later. It wasn't until I had finished my twentieth phone call and dispatched my eleventh bulletin to an insatiable Press that Mr. Washburn phoned me to say that the inquest had been held without excitement and that I had better get over to the funeral home on Lexington Avenue where Ella Sutton was to make her last New York appearance.

All the principals were there when I arrived, including the photographers. Eglanova wore the same black lace dress and white plumped hat that she had worn the day before and she looked very cool and serene, like a figure carved in ice. Louis had broken down and put on a blue suit and a white shirt, but no tie . . . while Alyosha, Jed Wilbur and Mr. Washburn all managed to look very decorous indeed. Miles looked awful, with red gritty eyes and a curiously blotched face. His hands shook and once or twice during the ceremony I thought he would faint . . . now just what was wrong with him? I wondered. He seemed not always to remember where he was and several times he yawned enormously . . . one photographer, quicker and less reverent than his fellows, snapped Miles in the middle of a yawn, getting the picture of the week for, when they ran it the next day, the newspapers commented: husband of murdered star enjoying a joke at funeral. I don't need to say that everything connected with the death of Ella Sutton was in the worst possible taste and, consequently, we had the most successful season in the history of American ballet.

The service was brief, inaccurate and professional. When it was over, the casket and at least a ton of flowers were carried out of the room by four competent-looking young thugs in ill-fitting cutaways and the long journey to Woodlawn began, three limousines transporting the funeral party. If Ella had had any family they did not choose to appear and so she was buried with only her ungrieving husband and her professional associates at her grave. I must admit that there are times when I hate my work, when I wish that I had gone on and taken my doctorate at Harvard and later taught in some quiet university, lecturing on Herrick and Marvell, instead of rushing about with side shows like this, trying to get the freaks in to look at some more freaks. Well, another day another dollar as the soldiers in the recent unpleasantness used to remark.

'How is the investigation coming?' I asked Mr. Washburn as we drove back to town; Alyosha sat silently on the back seat with us while two girl soloists sat up front with the driver.

'I'm afraid I'm not in Mr. Gleason's confidence,' said Mr. Washburn easily. 'They seem very busy and they seem quite confident . . . but that's all a part of the game, I'm told . . . to pretend they know who it is so that the guilty party will surrender. Not that I, for one minute, think any member of the company is involved.'

Mr. Washburn's unreality had a wonderfully soothing effect on me; I responded just like a prospective patron.

We both were rudely jolted out of this quiet mood when, upon arriving at the theater, a plainclothes man announced that Gleason would like to see me. I exchanged a startled glance with Mr. Washburn who turned visibly grey, thinking no doubt of those shears, of Eglanova's being involved in a scandal, of no season this fall because of no star.

Gleason, smoking a slobbery, ill-smelling cigar, looked every inch a Tammany man. His secretary sat at another desk, shorthand pad before him.

'Come in, Mr. Sargeant.' Oh, this was bad I thought.

'How are you today, Mr. Gleason?'

'I have some questions I want to ask you.'

'Anything you want to know,' I said graciously.

'Why didn't you mention at our previous interview that you had handled those shears?'

'What shears?'

'The Murder Weapon.'

'But I don't remember handling them.'

'Then how do you explain the fact that your fingerprints are on them . . . yours and no one else's?'

'Are you sure they're my fingerprints?'

'Now look here, Sargeant, you're in serious trouble. I suggest for your own good you take a more constructive attitude about this investigation or . . .' He paused, ominously, and I saw in my mind's eye the rubber hose, the glaring Klieg lights and finally a confession thrust under my bloody hand for that shaky signature which would send me to the gates of heaven for the murder of a ballerina I had ever known, much less killed. It was too terrible.

'I was just asking, that's all. I mean you never did fingerprint me . . .'

'We have ways,' said the Inspector. 'Now what were you doing with those shears between dress rehearsal and the murder?'

'I wasn't doing anything with them.'

'Then why . . .'

'Are my fingerprints on them? Because I picked them up off the floor and put them on top of the tool chest.'

Gleason looked satisfied. 'I see. And are you in the habit of picking up tools off the floor—is that your job?'

'No, it's not my job, but I *am* in the habit of picking things up . . . I'm very neat.'

'Are you trying to be funny?'

'I don't know why you keep accusing me of trying to amuse you . . . it's the last thing I'd try to do. I'm just as serious about this as you are. More so, because this scandal could louse up the whole season,' I added, piously, speaking the language of self-interest which men of all classes and nations understand.

'Then will you kindly explain why you happened to pick up The Murder Weapon and place it on that tool chest.'

'I don't know why.'

'But you admit that you did?'

'Of course . . . you see I stepped on them and almost fell,' I lied: how many years for perjury? threescore and ten; can I get there by amber light? yes, and back again.

'Now, we're getting somewhere. Why did you step on them?'

'Don't you mean where?'

'Mr. Sargeant . . .'

I spoke quickly, cutting him short, 'I'm not sure just where I was.' (This uncertainty might save me yet, I thought, watching that grim youth take down my testimony . . . well, I wasn't under oath yet.) 'Somewhere near the dressing rooms. I damn near fell. Then I looked down and saw those things at my feet and so I picked them up and put them on the box.'

'What time was this?'

'About ten-thirty.'

'*After* the murder?'

'Well, yes.'

'Didn't you think it peculiar that a pair of shears should be lying out in the open like that?'

'I had other things on my mind.'

'Like what?'

'Well, Ella Sutton, for instance . . . she had been killed a few minutes before.'

'And you made no connection between the shears and her death?'

'Of course not. Why should I? For all we knew at the time, the cable might have broken by itself.'

'When you did discover that the cable had been cut, why didn't you tell me at our last interview that you had handled The Murder Weapon?'

'Well, it just slipped my mind.'

'That is no answer, Mr. Sargeant.'

'I'd like to know what you want to call it then?' I was getting angry.

'Do you realize that you could be under suspicion right now for the murder of Ella Sutton?'

50

'I don't realize any such thing. In the first place you'll find that my fingerprints are on the cutting end of the shears, not the handle . . . also the fact that there are no other prints on it means that whoever *did* cut the cable had sense enough to wipe the shears clean.'

'How do you know there were no other prints?'

'Because you said there weren't . . . and, in case you still aren't convinced, I may as well tell you that I had less motive than anyone in the company for killing Sutton. I told you I didn't know the woman, and that's the truth.'

'Now, now,' said the Inspector with a false geniality that made his earlier manner seemed desirable by comparison. 'Don't get hot under the collar. I realize that you had no motive . . . we've checked into all that. Of course it doesn't do your girl friend any harm, having Ella Sutton gone, but that of course would hardly be reason enough for murder . . . *I* realize that.'

He was playing it dirty now but I said nothing; he had no case and he knew it. He was only baiting me, trying to get me to say something in anger which I would not, under other circumstances, say . . . something about Miles or Eglanova, or whoever they suspected. Well, I would disappoint him; I composed myself and settled back in my chair; I even lit a cigarette with the steadiest hand since the 4-H Club's last national convention.

'What I would like to know, though, is the exact position of the shears, when you first stumbled over them.'

'That's hard to say. The north end of the stage, near the steps which go up to the dressing rooms.'

'Whose rooms are there?'

'Well, Sutton's was, and Eglanova's, and the girl soloists share a room. The men are all on the other side.'

'Tell me, Mr. Sargeant, who do *you* think killed Ella Sutton?' This was abrupt.

'I . . . I don't know.'

'I didn't ask you if you knew . . . we presume you don't know. I just wondered what your hunch might be.'

'I'm not sure that I have one.'

'That seems odd.'

'And if I did I wouldn't be fool enough to tell you . . . not that I don't want to see justice triumph and all that, but suppose my guess was wrong? . . . I'd look very silly to the person I'd accused.'

'I was just curious,' said Gleason, with that same spurious air of good fellowship and I suddenly realized, like a flash, that, motive or not, I was under suspicion . . . as an accomplice after the fact or during the fact or even before it for all I knew. Gleason was quite sure that I was, in some way, on the murderer's side.

This knowledge froze me and the rest of our talk was mechanical. I do remember, however, wanting to ask him why he hadn't arrested Miles Sutton yet. It was very strange.

III

'AND then I told him that I thought I'd stumbled over the shears backstage, on my way to the dressing rooms.'

'Good boy,' Mr. Washburn was properly appreciative, having no reason yet to regret that favor he'd granted me the day before at the point of a gun or, rather, of a pair of shears.

'I wish, however, to record my serious unease, Mr. Washburn. I didn't like Gleason's questions. Just between us and the *New York Globe* he is about to pull something.'

'But, my dear boy, that's what he's paid for. He will have to make an accusation soon or the city will be angry with him. That's the price of office.'

'I think he suspects *me*.'

'Now don't be melodramatic. Of course he doesn't.'

'I don't mean of the murder, but . . . well, of being connected with it. My story about finding what is officially known as The Murder Weapon just didn't go down. He knows it was left some place else.'

'You don't think . . .' My employer looked alarmed.

'I just don't know.' And we left it at that.

On the way back to the office, I stopped off at Eglanova's Fifty-second Street apartment. She had invited me to come see her and I knew that she was always at home to those she liked, which was almost anyone who would pay a call to her.

She had the whole second floor of a brownstone to herself; it had been her home for twenty years and, consequently, it seemed now like a room from a Chekhov play: Czarist Russian in every untidy detail, even to the bronze samovar and the portraits of the Czar and Czarina, signed, on the piano, a grand affair, covered with an antique lace shawl and decorated with several more silver-framed photographs, of Karsavina, Nijinski and Pavlova. 'They are my family,' Eglanova was accustomed to say to casual visitors, waving her long sinewy hand at the photographs, including the Russian Royal Family as well as the dancers. Over the mantel was the famous painting of Eglanova in *Giselle*, her greatest moment in the theater . . . 1918.

Her maid opened the door and, without comment, ushered me into the presence.

'It is Peter!' Eglanova, wearing an old wrapper, sat by the bay window near the piano, looking out at a bleak little garden in the back where one sick tree grew among the tin cans and torn newspapers. She put down the copy of *Vogue* she was reading and gave me her hand. 'Come sit by me and keep me company.'

I sat down in a papier mâché Victorian chair and she said something in Russian to her maid who appeared, a moment later, from the kitchen with two ordinary drinking glasses full of hot tea and lemon. 'It is just right thing for hot day,' said Eglanova and we toasted each other gravely. Then she offered me some candy, rich creamy chocolates which made me sick just looking at them. 'All boys like candy,' she said emphatically. 'You sick maybe? or drink too much? American boys drink too much.'

I agreed to that all right . . . if anything causes this great civilization of ours to fall flat on its face it will be the cocktail party. I thought of those eighteenth-century prints of Rowland-son and Gilray and Hogarth, all the drunken mothers and ghastly children wallowing in gin in the alleys . . . it makes you stop and think. I thought longingly for several seconds of a gin and tonic.

'I couldn't take class again today . . . too hot. I perish.' Contrary to vulgar legend the lives of great ballerinas are not entirely given up to a few minutes of graceful movement every night followed by champagne drunk out of their toeshoes till dawn, in the company of financiers . . . no, most of their time is spent in filthy rehearsal halls, inhaling dust, or else in class, daily, year in year out, practising, practising even after they are already prima ballerinas. It occurred to me, suddenly, irrelevantly, that Eglanova was the same age as my mother.

'I think Jane Garden is taking class this afternoon.'

'Such darling girl! I hear she is your *petite amie*. So good for both of you.'

'Oh sure . . . it's wonderful.' News travels fast, I thought.

'I'm so happy to see good children happy. Every night?'

'What?' for a moment I didn't understand; then I blushed. 'Except on Wednesday, I guess, when she's too tired.'

'Just like me!' Eglanova laughed, a wonderful deep peasant laugh.' My husband Alexey Kuladin (he was prominent lawyer in Russia before) could never understand about Wednesday . . . I tell him about matinee but he would say: what difference?' She chuckled; we drank tea and Eglanova asked me more questions about what Jane and I did and what my habits had been previous to our affair. I told her a number of stories, mostly true, and she loved them. She was like one of those old women you read about who brood over an entire village and are never shocked no matter what happens . . . good witches. She made everything seem completely natural which, of course, it is or should be . . . she even regarded Louis with delight. 'Where does he get the energy? where?' I had just told her about my run-in with him. 'He works hard most of the day and at performance. Then he goes out and he drinks, oh, like an American, or maybe Russian . . . then he picks up one tough boy; then maybe another later on, not counting the people in the theater. It is wonderful! Such vitality! So manly!'

I wasn't convinced of the manly end of it but then it all depends on how you look at such things . . . he certainly acts like a man and there may be, who knows, not much difference between nailing a boy to the bed and treating a girl in like manner; it's all very confusing and I intend one day to sit down and figure the whole thing out. It's like the poem of Auden's, one of whose quatrains goes:

> Louis is telling Anne what Molly
> Said to Mark behind her back;
> Jack likes Jill who worships George
> Who has the hots for Jack.

Kind of flip but the legend of our age. Anyway, it may all be a matter of diet.

Eglanova wolfed down a couple of chocolates; I tried to recall if she were married at the moment but when I attempted straightening out in my mind the various marriages and divorces and widowhoods, some known and others suspected, I found I could not remember even half the names, mostly Russian ones, of her husbands and protectors . . . as they used to call boyfriends in the wicked days before the First World War.

'She will be lovely dancer,' said Eglanova, her mouth full of chocolate.

'Jane? I think so, too.'

'She is warm . . . here.' Eglanova touched her liver, the source, she said, of a woman's deepest emotion. A man's was somewhere south of the liver and much less reliable as a center of intensity and artistic virtue.

'Do you like her in *Eclipse*?'

'Very much. So strong. Is bad ballet of course.'

'Bad?'

'Very bad. Just tricks. We do all those things in nineteen twenty. We groan and suffer on stage for not enough love. We act like machines. We did everything then. Now American boys think it modern. Ha!' She gestured scornfully, sweeping the copy of *Vogue* off on to the floor.

'When did you see it?'

'Last night only . . . I was in final ballet so I went around front.'

'Sutton did it well, too.'

Eglanova's face darkened. 'Such tragedy!' she murmured intensely.

'The funeral was pretty awful.'

'Disgusting! Miles is fool!'

'I guess he was too broken up to make much sense about the arrangements.'

'Broken up? But why? He loathed her.'

'Still . . . it's a terrible thing to have happen.'

'Ah!' She looked menacing. 'If ever woman needed murder she did. But Miles was fool.'

'Why?'

Eglanova shrugged. 'How can he get away? It is so obvious. I know . . . you know . . . they, the public, know.'

'But why don't the police arrest him?'

She spread her hands, yellow diamonds gleamed in dusty settings. 'It is like ballet. You go slow. You introduce themes. Male solo. Female solo. *Ensemble*. *Pas de deux*. They know what they must do.'

This unexpected coldness was too much for me. 'You sound as if you want him to be found out.'

'It is not what *I* want . . . no, he is fool. His only hope was they could not prove he did it. But they always can once they know. Today they almost did.'

'When?'

'This morning at the . . . what they call it?'

'Inquest?'

'What funny word! Yes, they make it clear they watch him. He will not conduct tonight . . . or ever!' she added . . . this time like a wicked witch placing a curse.

'You sound as if you hated him.'

'I? *I* hate Miles? He is best conductor I have had since Paris. I shall grieve when he is gone . . . you may be confident. No, I am angry with him. He wants to kill wife . . . fine! I am all for it . . . like nature: get rid of what does not make you happy. If he tell me first, if he comes to me for advice, I say, certainly go kill her but do it natural . . . so you won't be caught. What is point of getting rid of nuisance only to be put away yourself? I have contempt for bad artists. He is hysterical fool. He lose his head. She refuses to give him divorce so he rushes backstage and cuts cable. Then he *is* in trouble.'

'Perhaps he didn't do it?'

'Oh yes he did . . . Miles is only person who is big fool enough to do it that way. I push her out of window in fit of anger. Ivan or Alyosha would poison her. Jed Wilbur would shoot her . . . Louis he would strangle her. Psychology!' said Anna Eglanova, winking solemnly at me.

'You seem to have thought a lot about it.'

'Who has not? Remember I am the one who must dance with that assistant conductor leading the orchestra always two bars behind me who am *always* on beat. *I* am martyr to this man's foolishness.'

'Are you glad of the new season?'

Eglanova sighed, 'Ah, Peter, I am old, I think. Thirty-one years is a long time to do *Swan Queen*.'

'But you'll never retire?'

'They will carry me protesting from the stage!' she laughed. 'They will have to kill me, too. And I tell you one thing . . . no fall from a cable would break *these* tough bones!' and she slapped her thighs.

Alyosha Rudin, in a white suit, stood in the doorway, bowing. 'Shall I go away?' he asked gallantly.

'My old friend has caught me in a compromising situation! Defend your honor, Alyosha! challenge him! I demand it!'

He smiled and took my hand, forcing me gently back into my chair. 'Don't get up, I will sit here.' And he pulled up a deep leather chair and joined us by the bay window. 'I am too old for duels.'

'How he has changed!' mocked Eglanova.

'But only for the better, Anna, like you.'

'For that I give you chocolates.' He actually ate one, I saw, marveling at his constitution . . . in this heat a lettuce leaf seemed too heavy for my stomach.

'I have been with Miles,' said the old man. 'He is in terrible state. I think he will have a breakdown, or worse.'

'His own fault.'

'Be charitable, Anna.'

'I am not responsible for his condition. I told him six months ago to divorce Ella no matter what she said . . . go ahead, I say, you have one life; you don't live forever . . . go ahead, I say, and divorce her whether she likes it or not. What can she do? That's what I told him.'

'But, Anna, obviously she *could* do something otherwise he wouldn't have waited like this; and then . . .'

'Killed her! Such big fool!'

'We know no such thing.'

'Oh, we don't "know no such thing",' mocked Eglanova. 'Tell that to this fat and ugly man who smoked cigars . . . tell *him*.'

'I know it looks very bad.'

'Oh . . . but I forget. The little one . . .'

'Magda? Her family is with her. What more?'

'Ah, what more indeed!'

'Then you know about Magda?' They both looked surprised, as though I had suddenly asked where babies came from.

'There are no secrets here,' said Alyosha gently.

'And now, can you not understand why I am furious with that idiot? It is all right to kill the wicked, to kill oneself, but *not* to hurt an innocent, oh, that is not moral . . . I swear that is wrong . . . Alyosha, tell me, tell him, that it is wrong.'

'Sad . . . too sad,' murmured the old man, accepting tea from the maid.

'Has Miles been to see her?' I asked.

'I think so,' said Alyosha, 'as often as possible . . . but it's not been easy.'

'The police?'

Alyosha nodded. 'It is the end of Miles if they find out and they will certainly find out . . . something which is known to fifty people is hardly a secret.'

'The fool got desperate,' said Eglanova, pointing her feet. 'She would not free him and there was the other girl *enceinte* . . . such mess!'

'Why was he afraid to divorce Ella?'

'Who can tell,' said Alyosha uneasily.

'Who can tell? Ha! I can tell . . . in this room at least. She would have exposed him. *She* was capable of that . . . he told me once that she'd threatened to make public private things if there was divorce against her.'

'What private things?' I asked.

'Anna!' Alyosha's usually gentle voice was harsh and warning . . . the way it was at rehearsal when the *corps de ballet* was off.

'Why make such secret? It is obvious to all but a baby like this. Miles takes drugs . . . not little ones like so many music people, no, big ones, dangerous, expensive ones. The sort that will kill you. *I* should know. My husband Feodor Mihailovitch died from opium at the age of thirty. He was big man, bigger than you, Peter, but when he died he weighed five stone . . . how much is that? seventy pound!'

2

Miles Sutton was not at the theater that night. According to the note on the bulletin board, he was home, sick, and until further notice the orchestra would be under the direction of Rubin Gold, a bright nervous young man with insufficient experience and a regrettable tendency to follow the music instead of the dancers.

After taking care of my usual chores at the box office, getting all the movie stars in their seats and one thing or another, I went back to Jane's dressing room, my first glimpse of her since our hung-over morning.

She was just getting into her tights when I marched into the dressing room. 'Good God! You frightened me.'

'You don't expect your buddy to knock, do you—or send a note back?'

'Of course not.' She went on with her dressing in spite of a number of distracting things which I thought of to do to her just then, those little peculiarities of behavior which are always a lot of fun at the time but might look alarming to a man from Mars, or even to a man from the police department. 'I don't know why I'm so jittery,' she said. 'But I tell you I *know* something's going to happen.'

'You mean the cable?'

She yelped and looked at me furiously. 'Don't even *suggest* such a thing! No, I was thinking of Miles. Everybody says the police are ready to arrest him.'

'What's been puzzling me is why they didn't do it a long time ago.'

'I don't know . . . not enough evidence . . . oh, darling, I just feel awful.'

I had a brave masculine moment, holding her in my arms while she shuddered a bit and gave way to some healthy old-fashioned female nerves; then, remembering that she was a dancer and not a woman, she broke the clinch and began to paint her face.

'Did you see Magda today?' I asked.

She nodded. 'The poor thing's out of her mind . . . her family isn't much help either. They're very Boston and though they're perfectly nice to her you can see they think it's the end of the world, her carrying the bastard child of a murderer . . . oh, it *does* sound awful, doesn't it?' Intently, she placed a set of eyelashes in place.

'How come you never lose them?'

'Lose what?'

'Eyelashes . . . Sutton used to lose them every performance according to legend.'

Jane laughed. 'I thought you asked me why I never lost babies . . . I stick them on with a special mess . . . all the girls use it. Oh!' She turned around suddenly. 'Did I tell you that they are going to give me *Coppelia*?' This called for a number of congratulatory words and deeds and the time passed pleasantly until Jane had to go backstage and do a few pre-performance knee bends and pirouettes. I walked with her as far as the long wooden bar near the tool chest; then I left her.

I paused for a moment and watched Eglanova in *Giselle* . . . it's not my favorite ballet and it's certainly not my favorite role for her. I am told she was once very fine in it but now she seems coy and unconvincing, too old and wise-looking, too regal, to play the part of a girl gone soft in the head for love.

During the intermission, I headed for Sherry's, the bar upstairs at the Met, where I found Mr. Washburn taking his ease in the company of my old employer, Milton Haddock, who was his usual noble drunken self, dressed casually in tweeds, horn-rimmed spectacles (old school, pre-junior executive: they curved); he looked very distinguished in a sottish way.

'Wonderful to see you, Mr. Haddock!' I exclaimed, pumping his hand.

'Why, hello there, George. Haven't seen you in a long time.'

'Not since New Haven.'

He clutched at the clue. '*Streetcar Named Desire* wasn't it? I remember now. You were at that party afterwards . . . some party. The Scotch flowed like the Liffey.' And he swallowed some more of it since Mr. Washburn was providing some gratis.

'And to think this is the man I worked for for four years,' I said jovially to Mr. Washburn, regretting those three fours: after all it was *my* prose style which made Milton Haddock the trenchant critic he is today, the adder of the Rialto . . . or at least the garter snake of Forty-fifth Street.

'My God . . . it's Jim,' said Haddock, recognizing me at last. He patted my arm, spilling my drink in the process. 'Here . . . I'm sorry . . . let me fix it for you.' And he dried my sleeve and cuff with his handkerchief, after which he carefully folded the handkerchief and put it away . . . to suck on later, I decided, in case he ran out of the stuff in the flask.

'I don't suppose you two have seen each other in a long time,' said Mr. Washburn.

'Not in a coon's age,' said Mr. Haddock, looking at me fondly with those foggy blues eyes of his. 'Right in the middle of the news, too, aren't you, Jim? Wonderful place for a young man to be when a hot story breaks . . . and such a story! Falling sandbag kills opera star in the first act of *Lakmé* . . . one of the dullest operas, by the way, I have ever sat through. I mean if it

61

had to ruin an opera it might just as well have been that one, don't you agree, Mr. Bing?' At that point I gave Mr. Washburn the high sign and we quietly crept away while the dean of New York drama critics had a chat with himself about the relative merits of the great operas.

'Why didn't you warn me?' asked Mr. Washburn.

'How could I? I didn't even know you knew him . . . after all, he never covers the ballet.'

'He did a story on Ella, thought he'd come by and have a chat. Awful experience.' Mr. Washburn shuddered as we stood and watched the last half of *Eclipse* run smoothly to its spectacular end. The audience ate it up and, beside me in the dark, I could hear Mr. Washburn applauding.

Jed Wilbur met us backstage; he looked less harried than usual and I suppose that the success of his ballet had bucked him up considerably.

'It is very, very fine,' said Mr. Washburn, slowly, taking Wilbur's right hand in both of his and looking at him with an expression of melting admiration and wonder . . . the four star treatment.

'Glad you liked it,' said Jed, in his high thin voice. 'Glad *they* liked it, too. Did you see the notices the new girl, Garden, received? Gratifying, very gratifying.'

'She danced well . . . but the part! Ah, Jed, you have *never* made such a fine ballet before in your whole life.'

'It isn't bad,' said Wilbur with that freedom from modesty and the commoner forms of polite behavior which makes dance people so refreshing and, at times, so intolerable. 'I thought the *pas de deux* went well tonight.'

'Lyric!' exclaimed Mr. Washburn as though all words but that accurate one had failed him.

'But the *corps de ballet* was a little ragged, I thought.'

'They are not used to such dynamic work.'

'By the way, I'm ready to talk about the new ballet.'

'Have you really thought it out? . . . will it be ready by the time we open in Chicago?'

'I think so . . . I'm ready to begin rehearsals, if you are.'

'What music? Something old and classical, I hope. They are the best, you know, the masters.'

'A little piece by Poulenc . . . you'll have no trouble getting the rights.'

Mr. Washburn sighed, thinking of royalties to a living composer. 'My favorite modern,' he said bravely.

'I knew you'd be pleased. I'm calling the ballet *Martyr* . . . very austere, very direct.'

'Brilliant title . . . but it's not, well, political, is it? I mean this isn't the best time . . . you know what I mean.'

'Are you trying to censor me?' Jed Wilbur stood very straight and noble, nostrils flared.

'Now, Jed, you know I'm the last person in the world to do such a thing. Why, I put the artist's integrity ahead of everything . . . you know that, Peter here knows that.'

'Yes, sir,' I murmured.

'But what *is* it about, Jed?'

'Exactly what the title says.'

'But *who* is the Martyr?'

'A girl . . . It's all about a family.'

'Ah,' said Mr. Washburn, relieved. 'Marvelous theme . . . seldom done in ballet. Only Tudor, perhaps, has done it well.'

'This is better than Tudor.'

'I'm sure it is.'

'What happens in the ballet—what's the argument?'

'It's very simple,' said Jed Wilbur, smiling. 'The girl is murdered.'

Mr. Washburn's eyebrows went up in surprise; mine went down in a scowl. 'Murdered? Do you think, under the circumstances, that's a . . . well, an auspicious theme for this company?'

'I can always take it to the Ballet Theater.'

'But, my dear boy, I wasn't suggesting you *not* do it, or that you change the theme. I was only suggesting that, perhaps, in the light of recent events . . .'

'It would be fabulous,' said the dedicated Mr. Wilbur, revealing an unexpected sense of the commercial for one so pure.

'Well, you're the doctor,' said Mr. Washburn jovially. 'Who will you need?'

'Most of the company.'

'Eglanova?'

'I don't think so . . . unless she would play the part of the girl's mother.'

'She wouldn't do it, I'm afraid. You can use Carole for that,

63

the heavy one . . . she's good in character. What about the girl?'

'Garden, I think,' said Wilbur, and I found myself liking him: what a break this would be for Jane—to have a new ballet made for her by a choreographer like Jed Wilbur! Things were looking up. 'I'll need all the boys. Louis can be her husband . . . a very good part for him, by the way . . . lot of fire. Then there are two brothers and her father. One brother plays games with her . . . they have, as children, an imaginery world all their own. The boy is a dreamer and he loses her to the other brother who is a man of action who loses her at last to Louis. But, of course, all the time, she belongs to her father (a good part for old Kazanian by the way) and her mother hates her. When she marries Louis there is terrible trouble in the family . . . a little like Helen of Troy, perhaps, and, to end the trouble, the girl is murdered.'

'Who murders her?' asked Mr. Washburn.

'The father, of course,' said Jed Wilbur evenly.

Neither of us said anything for a moment. Then Mr. Washburn chuckled. 'Obscure motivation, isn't it?'

'No, very classical . . . guilt, jealousy, incest.'

'Wouldn't he be more inclined to kill the girl's husband?' I suggested, appalled at the implications.

'He was a rational man . . . he realized that the boy was only fulfilling his nature . . . the boy had no connection with him; the girl had; the girl betrayed him *and* the brothers . . . the mother, too.'

'I'll be very interested to see how you work this out,' said Mr. Washburn with greater control than I would have had, similarly confronted.

'By the way,' I said to Wilbur, 'the *Globe* wants to know if you have any statement to make about this Communist deal.'

'Tell them I'm not a Communist . . . that two boards have cleared me already.' Wilbur seemed more relaxed now and I wondered why . . . after all, the pickets were at this very moment marching up and down the street outside with placards denouncing not only him but us. We found out soon enough. 'I've been signed to do the new Hayes and Marks musical this fall. . . . You can tell the *Globe* that.' And Mr. Wilbur marched off in the direction of Louis' dressing room.

'I guess that clears him,' I said. Hayes and Marks, sometimes known collectively as Old Glory, are the most successful, the most reactionary musical comedy writers on Broadway. To be hired by them is a proof of one's patriotism, loyalty and professional success.

'The little bastard,' said Mr. Washburn, lapsing for the first time in my brief acquaintance with him, into the argot of the street. 'I knew there'd be trouble when I hired him. I was warned.'

'What difference does it make? You've got at least one good ballet out of him and by the time you open with *Martyr* in New York next year the whole scandal will be forgotten. From what I heard the police are going to arrest Miles any minute.'

'I wonder why they don't?' mused Mr. Washburn, suggesting also for the first time that a member of his company might, after all, have been guilty of murder. It was obvious this exchange with Wilbur had shaken him.

'I know why,' I said boldly.

'You know?'

'It's those shears . . . they aren't sure about them . . . they can't figure what my role in all this is.'

'I'm sure that's *not* the reason.'

'Then what is?'

'I don't know . . . I don't know.' Mr. Washburn looked worried as the dancers trooped noisily by, costumed for *Scheherazade*. 'Oh,' he said, as we both watched one blonde trick march past us, rolling her butt, 'Lady Edderdale is giving a party for the ballet tonight . . . just principals, no photographers, except hers, of course. You be there, too, black tie . . . right after the last ballet. I'm not so sure that it's a good policy to be going out to parties so soon after an accident, but she's much too important a patron to pass up.'

I was thrilled, I have to admit. She gives the best parties in New York . . . a Chicago meat heiress married to a title . . . I wondered idly if I might find myself a rich wife at the party—every wholesome boy's dream of heaven. Thinking of marriage, I asked Mr. Washburn whether Eglanova was married at the moment or not.

He laughed. 'She has a Mexican divorce at the moment . . . I know it for a fact because I helped her get it when we were playing Mexico City.'

'Who was she married to then?'

'Don't you know? I thought you would have noticed it in her biography . . . but, no, come to think of it, we haven't used it in the program for nearly five years. She was married to Alyosha Rudin.'

IV

ONCE a Lady always a Lady, as the saying goes; especially in the case of Alma Shellabarger of Chicago who married the Marquis of Edderdale when she was twenty and then at twenty-four married someone else and after that someone else and so on until now, at fifty, she had no husband, though she still uses the title of Marchioness in spite of all the other names she has been called along the way. No one seems to mind, however, because she gives great parties even though her income is not as large now as it was when she appeared in the fashionable world with a face like a bemused horse and all that Shellabarger cash, from slaughtered pigs and sheep. Nevertheless, her blood-drenched income is adequate . . . though there is no longer the Paris house or the Amalfi villa or the Irish castle . . . only the Park Avenue mansion and the Palm Beach house, where lavish parties are given, in season. I am told that at her dinners neither pig nor sheep is served, only poultry, fish and game . . . real sense of guilt as any analyst would tell you at the drop of a fee.

Mr. Washburn and I arrived before the rest of our company. As a rule, he waits until Eglanova is ready and then he escorts her; but tonight, for some reason, he couldn't wait to get out of the theater. Both of us were hot in our tuxedos . . . his white and mine black, an obvious clue to our respective incomes. Fortunately, the house was cool . . . a gust of freshened air met us in the downstairs hall, a vast room with grey marble columns, marble floor and Greek statuary in niches. A footman took our invitations and led us up a flight of stairs where, so help me, a butler announced our names to a hundred or so decorative guests in a drawing room which looked like the waiting room at Penn Station redecorated by King Midas . . . the guests looked as though they might be waiting for trains, too, I thought, as we moved toward our hostess who stood beneath a chandelier at the room's center, all in green and diamonds, receiving her guests with a half-smile and mumbled greetings as though she weren't quite sure why she was there, or why *they* were there.

'Dear Alma,' said Mr. Washburn, beginning to expand as he always does in the presence of money.

'Ivan!' They embraced like two mechanical toys, like those figures which come out of old-fashioned clocks every hour on the hour. I bowed over her hand in the best Grand Saint Petersburg Ballet style.

'You poor dear,' said Alma, fixing my employer with yellow eyes. 'What a disaster!'

'We must take the good with the bad,' said Mr. Washburn gently.

'*I* was there!' breathed Alma Edderdale, shutting her eyes for a moment as though to recall, as vividly as possible, every detail of that terrible night.

'Then you know what it was like . . .'

'I do . . . I do.'

'The ghastly fall . . .'

'Can I ever forget?'

'The end of a life . . . a great ballerina's life.'

'If there was only *something* one could do.' That did it, I thought. Mr. Washburn would immediately suggest an Ella Sutton Memorial Ballet, sets, costumes and choreographer's fee to be paid by that celebrated patroness, the Marchioness of Edderdale. But Mr. Washburn is as tactful as he is venal.

'We all feel that way, Alma.' Then he paused significantly.

'Perhaps . . . but we'll talk of that another time. Tell me about *him*.'

'About whom?'

'The husband. The . . . well, you know what they say.'

'Ah . . . quite broken up,' said Mr. Washburn evasively, and I withdrew, moving toward the bar in the next room where, among other things, they were serving a Pommery '29 worth its weight in uranium. I knocked off two glasses before Jane arrived, looking very young and innocent in a plain white dinner dress, her hair drawn severely back ballerina-style. She was like the daughter of a country minister at her first grown-up party, only she looked perhaps too innocent to be the real thing. She caused a mild stir, her appearance at least: this gang hadn't absorbed her yet, made her a legend the way they had Eglanova who now stood, between Alyosha and Louis in

68

the doorway, like some bird of paradise poised on the edge of a hen coop. In the excitement of Eglanova's entrance, Jane and I met near the bar and toasted one another in Pommery.

'How did you like it tonight?' she asked, breathless and young, like a bride in an advertisement (and, like the model in question, well paid for her characterization).

'Wonderful party,' I said, enjoying myself for the first time, publicly at least, since my wild ballet season began. 'Best stuff I've ever tasted. And the air-conditioning! Wonderful job . . . like an autumn day.'

'You misunderstood,' said Jane firmly, with the bright monomaniacal stare of a dancer discussing the Dance. 'I meant my performance.'

'I'm afraid I didn't catch it. I was at the office most of the night, before I came here.'

She rallied bravely. 'You . . . *didn't* see me tonight?'

'No, I had to get some pictures off to the papers . . . the new ones of you, by the way,' I added.

'I got eight curtain calls.'

'That's my girl.'

'And three bouquets . . . from strangers.'

'Never take candy from strange men, little girl,' I chanted as we moved toward a tall French window which looked out on an eighteenth-century garden, all of five years old.

'I wish you'd seen it. Tonight was the first night I really *danced*, that I forgot all about the variations and the audience and that damned cable . . . that I really let go. Oh, it was wonderful!'

'You think you're pretty good, huh?'

'Oh, I didn't mean that!' She was anxious: nowadays in the theater good form (or actors' notion of good form) is everything. Everyone dresses carefully and quietly, no practical jokes, no loud voices and, above all, no reference to self . . . just smile and blush if you are congratulated for having won a Donaldson Award, look blank when someone mentions the spread on you in *Life*, murmuring something about not having seen it yet. In a way, I prefer the grand old egotists like Eglanova: she hardly admits that there is another ballerina in all the world . . . and even Louis has been known to ask reviewers:

'Who is this Youskevitch you talk to me about?' But anyway Jane had a storm of modesty which quickly passed and then, the Dance taken care of for the rest of the evening, we cruised the party.

About one o'clock we separated with an agreement to meet back at her apartment at two-thirty on the dot. Neither of us is very jealous . . . at least not in theory, and I wandered about the drawing room, saying hello to the few people I knew. I was pretty much lost in this crowd. It's not the gang I went to school with, the sons of those dull rich families who seldom entertain and who traipse off to Newport, Southampton, Bar Harbor and similar giddy places this time of year; nor is it the professional newspaper and theater world wherein I sing for my supper . . . rather, it is the world of unfixed money: obscure Europeans, refugees from various unnamed countries, the new-rich, the wilder old-rich, the celebrated figures in the arts who have time for parties and finally the climbers, mysterious and charming and busy, of all ages, sexes, nationalities, shapes and sizes. It takes a long time to straighten everybody out. I haven't even begun to see my way clear yet but I probably will in a few more years. Some people of course never do add things up right. Lady Edderdale is still among the more confused, after thirty years of high life.

Beneath a portrait of the lady of the house (the work of Dali) stood Elmer Bush with whom I have a nodding acquaintance . . . through no fault of mine I am not his bosom buddy: his column, 'America's New York,' is syndicated in seventy-two newspapers as well as being the *New York Globe's* biggest draw on the subway circuit. He was of course too important ever to visit the office, so the only time I met him was at first nights when he would always come up to Milton Haddock and say: 'It looks like a bomb from where I sit. What do *you* think, boy?' and Milton would grumble a little and sometimes I would be introduced and sometimes not.

'Hello there, Mr. Bush,' I said with more authority than usual since I was, after all, sitting in the middle of the best piece of news in town.

'Why if it isn't old Pete Sargeant himself,' said Mr. Bush, his face lighting up as he saw his next column practically composed already. He gave a polite but firm chill shoulder to a blonde middle-aged star of yesteryear who had obviously got the Gloria Swanson bug; then we were alone together in the middle of the party.

'Haven't seen you in a coon's age!' said Elmer Bush, showing a row of capped teeth: he has the seventh highest Hooper in television with a program called 'New York's America' which is, they tell me, a combination of gossip and interviews with theater people. . . . I never look at television myself because it hurts my eyes. Anyway, Elmer is big league, bald and ulcerous, the perfect symbol of metropolitan success for an earnest hard-working boy like me trying to get ahead in 'the game.'

'Well, I've been pretty busy,' I allowed in my best bumpkin manner.

'Say, what about that murder you got in your company?' and the benign features of Elmer Bush ('just a friend of the family in your own living room giving you some *real* stories about *real* people in the news,' . . . just old horse-shit Bush, I thought) shone with friendship and interest.

'Some mess,' I said, because that's exactly what he would have said had our roles been reversed.

'Well, it keeps the show in the news . . . that's one thing. Hear my broadcast about it Wednesday night?'

'I certainly did,' I lied. 'Just about the best analysis I've seen so far.'

'Well, I didn't really try to analyze it . . . just straight reporting.'

Had I blundered? 'I mean the way you put it, well, that was some job . . .'

'Get the facts,' said Mr. Bush, smiling mechanically. 'When are they going to arrest the husband?'

'I don't know.'

'He *did* do it?'

'Everyone thinks so. He certainly had a good enough reason.'

'Bitch?'

'Very much so.'

'I saw the man who's on that case yesterday. What's his name? Gleason? Yes. Used to know him years ago when I was covering the police courts. He was mixed up in the Albemarle business . . . but that was before your time. Anyway, he made it pretty clear to me, unofficially of course, that Sutton would be arrested in the next twenty-four hours and indicted as quick as possible . . . while public interest is high. That's the way they work.' And he chuckled. 'Politicians, police . . . the worst hams of all. But I still don't know why they've held off so long.'

'Pressure,' I said smoothly, as though I knew.

He pursed his lips and nodded, everything just a bit more deliberate than life, made sharp for the television camera. 'I thought as much. Not a bad idea to string it out as long as possible either . . . for the good of all concerned. Are you sold out? I thought so. Take a tip from me! *This* will put ballet on the map.' And with that message he left me for a dazzling lady who looked like Gloria Swanson and who, upon close inspection, turned out to be Gloria Swanson.

'How're you doing, Baby?' inquired a familiar voice behind me . . . needless to say I gave a bit of a jump and executed a fairly professional pirouette . . . never turn your back on the likes of Louis, as Mother used to say.

'I'm doing just fine, killer,' I said, showing my upper teeth.

'Such good boy,' said Louis, holding my arm for a minute in a vice-like grip. 'Some muscle!'

'I got it from beating up faggots in Central Park,' I said slowly; he doesn't understand if you talk fast.

Louis roared. 'You kill me, Baby.'

'Don't tempt me.'

'Come on out on that balcony . . . just you and me. We look at moon.'

'Not on your life, killer.'

'Why're you so afraid of me?'

'Just two guesses.'

'But I tell you you won't feel nothing. You'll like it fine.'

'I'm a virgin.'

'I know, Baby, that's what I go for. Last night . . .' But before he could tell me some lewd story concerning his unnatural vice, Jed Wilbur approached us, pale and harried-looking, like the White Rabbit in *Alice in Wonderland*. He too was got up in a dinner jacket . . . it was the first time, I think, that I had ever seen him in a suit, wearing a tie. I was not able to continue my sartorial investigation, however, for Louis broke off what had promised to be our big balcony scene and rushed off in the direction of the main hall, as though he had to get to the john real fast. I could see that Wilbur was in some doubt as to whether to chase his beloved and corner him in some barricaded lavatory or to tarry a bit with me instead. He chose the latter course.

'I wonder where Louis is off to?' he asked.

'Call of the wild, I guess.'

'What was he talking to you about?'

This was abrupt and I was almost tempted to remind Jed Wilbur that it was none of his business. But then he is the leading choreographer of the minute and I am, for this minute at least, a minion of the ballet and so I swallowed my thimble-sized pride and said, 'Just idle chatter.'

'In other words making a pass.' Wilbur sounded bitter.

'But that's natural. I mean for him it is. He has to get into everything he sees.'

'Male and under thirty.' Wilbur sighed and I felt sorry for him . . . unrequited love and all that. He fidgeted with his ready-tied bow tie.

'Well, that's the way he gets his kicks,' I said, idly dropping into an Army attitude; while I talked to Jed I looked over his shoulder at the room, recognizing several famous faces, one of whom, belonging to a Senator, was talking very seriously to Jane who obviously had no notion of who he was. I smiled to myself as I recalled the day before when she asked me, very tenderly and shyly, whether Truman was a Democrat or Republican.

'Why does everyone at parties look over everyone else's shoulder?' asked Wilbur suddenly, capturing my attention with a bang.

'Oh . . .' I blushed. 'Bad manners, I guess.'

'*Some* commentary on our society,' said Wilbur, in a voice which smacked a little of the soapbox. 'Everyone trying to get ahead every minute of the day . . . rushing, rushing, rushing, afraid of missing a trick.'

'This is a competitive town,' I said with my usual profundity, sneaking a glimpse over *his* shoulder at Eglanova who was surrounded by some rich-looking bucks, laughing as though she was quite prepared to slip off a shoe and guzzle champagne from it.

'You're telling me,' said Wilbur and he looked over his own shoulder in the direction that Louis had taken . . . but our Don Juan was nowhere in sight. No doubt he was having his way

73

with one of the busboys behind a potted palm downstairs. Thinking of Louis always puts me into a good mood . . . that is when he's not around to make me nervous . . . he just makes me laugh, for no particular reason. But then Lady Edderdale, surrounded by outriders, rode down on us, diamonds whispering against green satin.

'Mr. Wilbur? We haven't met. I must have been in the other room when you arrived. I've so much wanted to meet you.'

Jed took her outstretched hand, bewildered. 'Yes . . .'

'*I* am Alma Edderdale,' she said, smiling a blinding smile, like sun on a glacier; she withdrew her hand.

'We've met,' I said quickly, to cover the moment's confusion. 'With Mr. Washburn.'

'Of course. Can I ever tell you in words, Mr. Wilbur, my reaction to *Eclipse*?'

Wilbur suggested in a confused voice that she give it a try . . . stated more politely of course.

'It was my one wonderful, *mystical* experience in the ballet . . . not including the classics which I have seen so long that I can no longer remember how they first affected me. But in *modern* ballet . . . ah!' Words failed her. They failed Jed, too.

'It's generally thought to be Mr. Wilbur's best work,' I gabbled.

'And of course what happened that first night! Mr. Wilbur, *I* was there. I saw.' She opened her eyes very wide, great golden orbs, swimming in jaundiced tears.

'Very awful,' mumbled Wilbur.

'And to have had it happen then . . . at that wonderful moment! Ah, Mr. Wilbur . . .' The passage of several boisterous guests made escape possible; I slipped through them and wandered off to find Jane. But she had vanished . . . the Senator, too. I settled for Eglanova who was seated on a love seat with an old man and surrounded by younger ones, all rather sensitive I noted with my shrewd and merciless eyes . . . I can tell one of our feathered friends at twenty paces: a certain type anyway. The Louis kind nobody can spot until they're coming at you . . . then flight is in order, if they're bigger than you.

'My darling Peter!' Eglanova was mildly lit, not yet weepy and Czarist the way she gets when she is really gone on vodka

. . . twice a year: at Russian New Year and backstage the last night of every season in New York . . . her *last* season, she always moans, so they say. She gave me her hand to kiss and, feeling good on all the Pommery I had drunk, I kissed it soulfully.

'I have had such good time with young men.' She waved to include them all. They giggled. 'I never go home now.'

'It's late, Anna,' said Alyosha, suddenly joining us.

'Tyrant! Tomorrow I do one *pas de deux* . . . no more.'

'Even so.' Then he spoke in Russian and she answered in Russian, both speaking rapidly, seriously, the good humor of the party-mood gone, I thought. Eglanova's face went quite pale though it was impossible to tell since her make-up was like spar varnish . . . perhaps, it was the way her eyes opened very wide and her face fell, literally sagged, as though whatever force had been holding it tight across the bone suddenly gave way. Then, with a stage gesture, she got up, swept a half-curtsy to her admirers and, without saying a word to any of us, left the room on Alyosha's arm. I saw them at the door saying good night to Lady Edderdale.

I looked about the room for Jane but she was gone. I wondered if she had gone home early . . . or perhaps had decided in a puckish mood to have a Senatorial fling. Well, she could look out for herself, I decided, and went downstairs to the bathroom. I was just about to go in when I saw Mr. Washburn come trotting across the black and white marble floor.

'I was looking for you,' he said, stopping short, breathing hard. 'We've got to get out of here.'

'Why? What's the matter?'

'I'll tell you outside. Come on.' He looked furtively about as though afraid the footmen were eavesdropping. They were not. Even so, as we went out the door, he looked back over his shoulder, like a man fearing pursuers; I looked, too, and saw no one except Louis coming out of the head with a blond footman, both looking pleased as hell. They did not see us.

We headed east on Seventy-fifth Street, toward Lexington Avenue.

'What's going on? What's up? Where're we walking to?'

'It's quicker, walking,' said Mr. Washburn grimly, prancing ahead of me like a fat mare.

'But where?'

'To Miles Sutton's apartment. He lives just the other side of Lexington.'

'What's the matter?' But I knew: Gleason had arrested him at last, or was about to.

'He's dead,' said Mr. Washburn.

I think I said: 'Sweet Jesus!'

2

We walked up three flights of stairs which smelled of damp and cabbage; at the top of the third flight was an open door with a curiously formal card on it: 'Mr. and Mrs. Miles Sutton' . . . obviously a Christmas present from an old aunt. The apartment was a three-roomed affair, very modern: you know the kind . . . two walls battleship grey and two terra cotta in the same room with fuchsia-covered furniture. This was where the happy couple had lived until the present season when Miles moved out, not returning until after Ella was dead.

In the front room several detectives stood, looking important as they always do in the presence of someone's else's disaster. They were very tough with us until Gleason, hearing the noise of Mr. Washburn's protests, shouted from another room, 'Let them in.'

'In there,' said one of the detectives, motioning to a door on the left.

We found Gleason in the kitchen. A photographer with a flash bulb was taking pictures of the corpse, from all angles. Two unidentified men stood by the sink, watching.

'Oh, my God!' And Mr. Washburn, after one look at the body of Miles Sutton, hurried out of the room. We could hear him vomiting in the bathroom. I didn't feel so good myself but I have a strong stomach and I have seen a lot of things in my time, during the war, and I'm not easily upset . . . even so all the wine I had drunk that night at the party turned sour in my belly as I looked at Miles Sutton. It was one of the damnedest things I have ever seen. He was slumped over a gas stove, his arms hanging at his sides and his legs buckled crazily under him . . . he was a tall man and the stove didn't come up to his waist. But the horrible thing was his head. He had fallen in such a way that his chin had got caught in one of the burners on top of the stove . . . which might not have been so bad except for the fact that the gas had been lit and his hair, his beard and the skin of his face were burned until now his head resembled a shapeless mass of black tar. The room was full of the acrid odor of burnt hair and flesh.

'O.K.,' said the photographer, getting down from a kitchen chair: he had been shooting a picture from directly overhead. 'It's all yours.'

The two men by the sink moved forward and lifted the body off the stove. I looked away while they lugged the large corpse out of the kitchen into the living room. Gleason and I, still without a word to one another, followed the procession into the living room.

A moment later Mr. Washburn joined us, very weak at the knees. Without further invitation, he sat down in an Eames chair, careful not to look at Miles Sutton who was now laid out on a stretcher in the middle of the room. Detectives scurried about, searching the room, taking photographs.

Gleason lit a cigar and glared at us.

'How . . . how did it happen?' asked Mr. Washburn in a low voice.

'It ruins the whole case,' said Mr. Gleason, savagely chewing on his cigar.

'Poor Miles . . .'

'It makes no sense.'

'Inspector, could you . . . would you *please* put something over him.'

'You don't have to look at it,' snapped Gleason, but he motioned to one of the detectives who found a sheet and covered the body.

'That's better,' said Mr. Washburn.

'We were going to arrest him this evening,' said Gleason. 'We had a perfect case . . . in spite of everyone's refusal to co-operate with us.' And he looked at me with bloodshot eyes . . . when Irish eyes are bleary, I hummed to myself.

'How could such a thing have happened? I mean . . . well, it's impossible.'

'That's our business: the impossible.'

'How could someone have got in that position ? . . . I don't understand.' Mr. Washburn sounded querulous.

'That's what we're going to find out . . . the medical examiner here,' he gestured to one of the men standing by the door, 'says that he's been dead for about an hour.'

'It must've been an accident,' said Mr. Washburn.

'We'll know after the autopsy. We're going to do a real job, you can bet your life. If there's been any monkey business we'll find out.'

'Or suicide,' suggested Mr. Washburn.

Gleason looked at him contemptuously. 'A man decides to kill himself by lighting a gas stove and putting his head on the burner like it was a pillow or something? For Christ's sake! If he was going to kill himself he would've stuck his head *in* the oven and turned on the gas. Anyway he was about to cook something . . . we found a pan beside him on the floor.'

'Unless somebody put it there . . . to make it look like an accident,' I suggested, to Mr. Washburn's dismay.

The detective ignored me, though. 'I wanted you to come here, Mr. Washburn, to tell me which members of your company were at the party tonight.'

'All the principals . . . Rudin, Wilbur . . . everyone.'

'Who?'

Mr. Washburn, unhappily, gave him all the names.

'Where was the party held?' When Mr. Washburn told him, Gleason whistled, putting two and two together in a manner marvelous to behold . . . there's nothing quite like watching a slow reflex in action.

'That's just a few blocks from here?'

'I believe so,' said Mr. Washburn.

'Anyone could have come over here and killed Sutton.'

'Now look here, you don't know he was killed . . .'

'That's right, but then I don't know it was an accident, either.'

'Just how could anybody kill a grown man by pushing his head on a stove?' I asked.

'It could be done,' said Gleason, 'if you knocked him out.'

'Is there any sign he was knocked out?' I asked.

'The examination hasn't been made yet. In the meantime, Mr. Washburn, I want you to have the following people ready to see me tomorrow afternoon at the theater.' And he handed my employer a list of names.

'How soon will you know . . . what happened, whether he was knocked out or not?'

'By morning.'

'Morning . . . oh, God, the papers.' Mr. Washburn shut his eyes; I wondered why publicity should bother him at this point.

'Yes, the papers,' said Gleason, irritably. 'Think what they'll say about *me?* "Suspect killed or murdered on eve of arrest." Think how that'll make *me* look!' I wondered if perhaps Gleason might not have political ambitions . . . Gleason for Councilman: fearless investigator, loyal American.

My reverie was broken, however, by the appearance of a dark, disheveled woman who pushed her way past the detectives at the door and then, catching sight of the figure on the floor, screamed and drew back. There was a moment of pure confusion. The woman was taken into a back room by the medical examiner who spoke to her in a low, soothing voice which had startlingly little effect on the sobs. Magda was hysterical.

'Was *she* at the party?' asked Gleason, turning to Mr. Washburn, the sobs muffled now by a closed door.

'No, no . . .' Mr. Washburn looked about distractedly, as though ready to make a run for it.

'She's been sick,' I volunteered.

'I know she has,' said Gleason. Then the sobbing stopped and presently the door to the bedroom opened and Magda, supported on one side by the doctor, joined us. Whatever shot the doctor had given her was obviously working like a charm for she was in complete control of herself now . . . even when she looked at the sheet-covered figure on the floor, she remained calm.

'Now,' said Gleason, in a voice which was, for him, gentle, 'why did you come here tonight?'

'To see Miles.' Her voice was emotionless; she kept staring at the white sheet.

'Why did you want to see him?'

'I . . . I was afraid.'

'Of what?'

'Of his being arrested. You were going to arrest him, weren't you?'

'He was guilty.'

She shook her head, slowly. 'No, he didn't kill her . . .but I told you that once, when you came to see me.'

79

'What did you intend to do tonight? Why did you come?'

'I wanted to . . . to get him to run away, with me, the two of us. We could have gone to Mexico . . . any place. I wanted . . .' But she didn't finish her sentence; she looked dully at Gleason.

'You couldn't have got away,' said Gleason quietly. 'He couldn't have got away. You see, he was watched every minute; didn't you know that? Why, there was even a man watching this building tonight.'

Mr. Washburn gave a start. 'You mean . . .'

Gleason nodded, looking very pleased with himself. 'I mean, Mr. Washburn, that at one-ten you were seen entering this building and at one-twenty-seven you left it, in a great hurry. What were you doing here?'

Mr. Washburn shut his eyes, like an ostrich heading for a sandpile.

'What were you doing here?'

'I came to talk to Miles.' Mr. Washburn opened his eyes and his voice was even and controlled: he was still the intrepid Ivan Washburn, the peerless impresario . . . he could take care of himself, I decided.

'And did you talk to him?'

'Yes, I did . . . and if you're implying that I killed him you are very much mistaken, Inspector Gleason.'

'I implied no such thing.'

'Don't even think it,' said Mr. Washburn, coolly, as though he were saying: if you go after me I'll see that you end up pounding a beat in Brooklyn. 'I had some business I wanted to talk over with Miles. That's all.'

'What kind of business?'

'His contract, if you must know. I told him that it would not be renewed. That we would tour without him.'

'What was his reaction to this?'

'He was upset.'

'Why did you tell him this tonight? Why didn't you have him come to your office tomorrow? Or you could have written him.'

'I wanted to tell him myself. He was a friend of mine, Mr. Gleason . . . a very good friend.'

'Yet you were prepared to fire him?'

'I was indeed.'

'Why?'

'Because I suspected that sooner or later you would arrest him and that, even if you didn't, too many people thought he was a murderer . . . too many of our backers, to be blunt about it.'

'I see . . . and you left in the middle of a party to come tell him this?'

'We both seem agreed that I did,' said Mr. Washburn.

'Could anyone else have visited Sutton this evening?' I asked, eager to get my employer off the hook.

Gleason ignored me. 'Did you notice anything unusual about the deceased?'

'He was not deceased when I arrived, if that's what you mean, and he was very much alive when I left.'

'I meant did he act peculiar in any way, say anything which might throw light on what subsequently happened?' Excellent sentence, Gleason, I said to myself; he was beginning to face up to the fact that none of his 'deceased' talk was going to get him anywhere with this gang.

'He objected to my firing him and he said that he did *not* kill his wife no matter what the police thought and that he would welcome a trial.'

'So he told us,' said Gleason. 'And we were perfectly willing to give him a chance to tell all, under an indictment, of course. But then what did you say?'

'I told him that I was convinced of his innocence, but that no one else was, that I would be only too happy to take him back *after* a trial, presuming he was acquitted.'

'You got the feeling, then, that Sutton was looking forward to a trial?'

'No, I didn't.'

'But you said . . .'

'As a matter of fact, he was terrified of appearing in court. As you know he took drugs and he was positive that the prosecution would throw all that at him . . . I *can* tell you that he was not afraid of the murder charge . . . I don't know why but he wasn't; it was the drug thing that disturbed him: the idea not only of being sent to jail for it, or whatever the law is, but, worse, of having it taken away from him even for a few days during the trial . . .'

'He was going to give all that up when we were married,'

said Magda in a tired, faraway voice. 'There's a place in Connecticut where they cure you. He was going to go there. We were to spend our honeymoon there.' She stopped abruptly, like a phonograph when the needle's lifted.

'Then when you left the . . . Sutton he was alive and angry.'

'I'm afraid so . . . angry, I mean.'

'Did anyone else come to see him in the last hour?' I repeated.

'*I'm* asking the questions,' snapped Gleason.

'Was that fire escape watched?' I asked, just to be ornery. 'The one outside the kitchen window.'

'So you noticed there was a fire escape, eh?'

'I did.'

'Were you at the party, too?'

'Yes . . . remember, Mr. Gleason, I'm the one without a motive.'

Gleason gave me a warning or two about the possible dangers into which my insouciance might yet lead me.

While we had been talking the detectives had ransacked the apartment and the photographer had taken pictures of everything in sight. They were now ready to push off. Gleason receiving a signal from his chief lieutenant, stood up, rubbing his hands together as though washing them of the guilt of others.

'I will see all of you, tomorrow. Can you get home alone?' He turned to Magda.

'Yes . . . yes,' she said, stirring in her chair.

'You better see her home, Macy.' The detective in question nodded and helped her to her feet.

'I hope,' said Mr. Washburn, 'that this turns out to be the end of the whole ugly business.'

'Or the beginning,' said Gleason darkly.

'I presume that you had a case against him. Now that he is dead . . . suicide, accident, who knows how he died? . . . the fact remains that a man about to be arrested for a murder has died and so the case . . . Oh, Lord, look!' Mr. Washburn leaped back and we all turned to stare at the figure on the floor. The sheet which covered him had caught fire from the still smoldering head and a yellow flame, like a daffodil in the wind, blossomed on the white sheet. I was not there, however, to see it put out; I had followed, as quickly as I could, Mr. Washburn's blind dash down the stairs to the street outside.

For once I didn't really want to see the newspapers; neither did my employer but of course we read them all, together, in absolute silence. 'Death Company' . . . 'Slain Dancer's Husband Suicide' . . . 'Mystery Death of Murder Suspect' . . . 'Second Death in Jinx Ballet' . . . Needless to say, we had all the front pages to ourselves. When we had finished the lot we looked at one another. Fortunately, at that moment, Alma Edderdale saw fit to telephone and I left the office and headed for the Met.

A crowd had gathered at the stage door, for no particular reason . . . just to be as near as possible to a couple of murders and, better yet, to be near a murderer. I pushed my way through them and went immediately to Jane's dressing room. She had been asleep when I got home from Sutton's apartment the night before and she had been asleep when I left in the morning, at nine o'clock, to help Mr. Washburn with the reporters who had, for three hours, made our lives miserable at the office.

She was mending one of her costumes; the day was cruelly hot and she wore no clothes.

I gave her a long healthy kiss, tilting her chair back so far that she kicked the air gracefully with her long legs, to keep her balance.

'Is it true?' she asked, when we were done and I was again composed.

I nodded. 'Has Gleason seen you yet?'

'I don't see him till four something. He killed himself, didn't he?'

'I suppose so.'

'But . . . like that! Did you see him?'

I shuddered, remembering. 'I'll say. It was the awfullest sight . . . worse than the war . . . at least then you were usually looking at people you didn't know, and there were so many of them . . .'

'But the papers act as if he'd been murdered.'

'I don't believe it.'

'But how could he kill himself in that way?'

'He might've passed out . . . you know he was taking an awful lot of the stuff, whatever it was he took . . . you remember my telling you how I found him passed out in the hall the day after Ella died.'

'Let's hope this is the end of the whole mess.'

'I hope so, too.' But I knew that we hadn't come to the end of the trouble . . . I'd taken to calling it 'the trouble' in my mind, like one of those Negro spirituals.

'How're the kids in the company holding up?'

'Scared to death,' Jane smiled. 'They're positive we've got a maniac around . . . they go everywhere in pairs, even to the john.'

'And the thing I always liked about dancers was that they had no imagination.'

'Sometimes I think you're against ballet.'

'I am . . . I am,' I said, locking the door. 'But I'm not against you . . .' And I headed for her with an insane leer, scaring hell out of her. Then, before she had time to complain, I was out of my clothes and we were together on the floor, doing it like Mamma and Poppa as Eglanova would say . . . she likes the old-fashioned, heart-to-heart method, with no thrashing about . . . so do I, on hot days at least, when anything else would use up too much energy. After we finished, we lay side by side for a bit on the cool dirty floor.

'We shouldn't have done that,' said Jane, at last.

'Why not? We missed last night. At least I did.'

'I did, too.'

'Are you sure you didn't have a frolic with that Senator?'

'With who?'

'That big middle-aged job with the grey hair you were talking to at the party . . . the red face.'

'Oh him! Was he a Senator?'

'I should say so.'

'He told me he was a broker named Haskell.'

'I hope you got your money in advance.'

'Don't be dirty.'

A knock on the door brought us both to our feet in a flash. 'Wait a second,' called Jane in the cool voice of one used to keeping her head in crises. Since I had not taken off my shoes and socks, I was able to dress with a speed which did credit to my military training. Jane slipped into a bathrobe and opened the door while I sat down before the dressing-table mirror and dried my sweaty face with a handkerchief as Magda entered.

'I'm sorry,' she said. 'I didn't know . . .'

'Come on in,' said Jane briskly, offering her the third and last chair. 'How do you feel?'

'Awful . . . naturally.'

'I thought you were too sick to come to the theater?'

'I am,' said Magda, and she did look ill. 'I wanted to come, though. To talk to you, to my friends here. You have no idea what it's been like this last week with my family around and everything, not being able to see Miles . . .' Her voice broke a little. 'The family wouldn't let me see him but he came once, anyway, when they were out and we talked and made plans and then went to see him last night.'

'Have you see Gleason yet today?' I asked quickly, before she could start weeping.

'Yes.'

'What does he say—what about the autopsy?'

'He wouldn't tell me but I told him that someone had killed Miles . . . I don't know how but someone did.'

'But why? If somebody else murdered Ella then they certainly wouldn't murder Miles just as he was about to be arrested for Ella's murder.'

'Oh, but they would,' said Magda. 'You see, Miles knew who killed Ella.' I must say this gave us both a jolt.

'How do you know he did?'

'Because he told me so the last time I saw him. He told me not to worry . . . that if they tried to charge him with murder he would tell everything.'

'But he didn't tell you who it was?'

Was it my imagination or did she pause just a second before she answered? Before she said, 'No, he didn't tell me.'

'Did you tell Gleason all this?'

'Oh yes . . . I told him a lot more, too.'

'The sooner it's finished the better,' said Jane emphatically, taking out her sewing kit and going to work on the torn costume.

We talked a little more and then, seeing that the girls had a lot to discuss, I wandered on stage where Alyosha was giving some directions to the electricians. He looked very dapper in a Lord Byron shirt, magenta slacks, with a silk handkerchief tied about his lean neck and his monocle screwed in one eye.

'We must have everything right for tomorrow,' he said to me as the electrician walked away. 'Anna will do *Swan Lake*.'

'And for once, it won't be her "last" performance,' I said.

Alyosha smiled. 'No, she won't be able to weep this year. Ten more years I give her. She is at her peak.'

Well, you better get her some contact lenses, I said to myself, trying to imagine the old star at sixty reeling about the stage in *Giselle*.

'Have you seen Wilbur today?'

I said that I hadn't.

'I was told he was to start rehearsing the new ballet today . . . if he is he should send out a call for the dancers he wants. They are all eager, naturally.'

'I think he intends to use most of the company, but not until the season closes.'

'If you see him, though, tell him to let me know which dancers he will want . . . he is not used to our system.'

I said that I would and we parted.

My interview with Gleason was more amiable than usual.

He looked very hot in a white crumpled suit which made me think of a photograph I once saw of William Jennings Bryan when he was down in Tennessee fighting evolution.

Where were you at such and such a time and did you for any reason leave the party before such and such an hour? No sir I did not sir. We got through the preliminaries without a blow. Then the first of the brass tacks.

'Where, Mr. Sargeant, did you find those shears?'

'I found them, now that I think of it, in Eglanova's dressing room . . . someone had put them in the wastebasket. I took them out.'

'Why didn't you tell us this before?'

'I wasn't sure it had any bearing on the case.'

'Aren't *we* to be the judges of that?'

'Certainly . . . I didn't remember at the time. So many things had happened.' I'm no fool . . . I've watched some of those investigations over television: all you have to do is say you can't remember, or that you've suddenly remembered, and you're legally safe.

'It might have made it easier for us if you'd been able to remember at the time.'

'Well, I didn't.'

'I wonder if you realize how serious all this is, Mr. Sargeant.' For some reason Gleason had decided to handle me with tenderness.

86

'I do. . . . It was a dumb thing, wasn't it? For someone deliberately to put the shears in her wastebasket to throw suspicion on her . . . I mean, if she *had* cut the cable she'd never keep The Murder Weapon in her own dressing room.'

'Very sound reasoning,' said the detective; if I hadn't already been acquainted with his simple mind I would have thought he was indulging himself in a bit of irony at my expense.

'What did the autopsy turn up?' I asked, disregarding all his previous statements to the effect that it was not my place to ask questions.

'If you would just let us . . .' He began with a show of patience.

'Mr. Gleason,' I lied, 'I have the representatives of all the wire services, foreign and domestic, as well as reporters from every daily in town, waiting at my office for some word from Anthony Ignatius Gleason as to the outcome of the autopsy this morning . . .' That did the trick . . . Gleason for Mayor, Honest, Courageous, Tireless.

'As a rule the district attorney's office handles releases to the Press but since the boys are so eager you can tell them that Miles Sutton had a heart attack and fainted, falling face forward on to the lighted stove. He was not attacked or poisoned . . . unless you can call a system which looked like a drugstore poisoned.'

'That's certainly a load off my mind,' I sighed. 'Everybody else's, too.'

'It would seem,' said Gleason, 'that the case is closed.'

'Seem? Weren't you going to arrest him for murder?'

'Oh yes.'

'He did kill her, didn't he?'

'We believe so.'

'Then tell me; why did you wait so long to arrest him? What couldn't you prove?'

Gleason blinked and then, quite mildly, answered, 'Well, it happened that of all the people involved Sutton was the only one who had an alibi . . . the only one who could not, if his story was true, have gone backstage between five and eight-thirty and cut the cable.'

I whistled.

'There are times when a good alibi can be more suspicious than none at all. But we managed to break it. I won't say how because we weren't entirely sure but we had a theory and we thought we could prove it in court.'

'Then I can tell the papers that the case is finished?'

Gleason nodded. 'You can tell them that.'

'They'll want to interview you.'

'They know where to find me,' he said quietly . . . Gleason for Governor, Man of the People.

Needless to say, my announcement to the Press that afternoon caused a sensation. Everyone in the company was wild with excitement and relief and I felt like a hero even though I was just the carrier of the good news from Aix to Ghent.

After the last reporter had cleared out of the office, grinding the last cigarette butt into the expensive carpet, I sat back and enjoyed a few minutes of much needed solitude. The two secretaries in the next room made a restful steady noise of typing: 'Miss Rosen and Miss Ruger, the talented duo-typists, made their Manhattan debut last night at Town Hall with a program which featured Samuel Barber's *Concerto for Two Typewriters with Black and Red Ribbons.*' I seldom get a chance to be alone any more . . . it wasn't like college or even the army when I would have long stretches of being by myself, when I could think things out, decide what to do next, figure just where I stood on any number of assorted topics like television, Joyce, deism, marionettes, buggery and Handel's *Messiah.* Maybe I should take a long rest . . . I'd saved up quite a bit of cash and . . . but my dream of solitude was shattered by a telephone call from Miss Flynn.

'I have had an inquiry from the Benjamin Franklin Kafka Foundation; they would like to know if you could handle their account for the next six months. I indicated that I would communicate with you.'

I asked what sum they had suggested and when she told me I said that I would accept. We talked business for a few minutes. Then she suggested that I come by the office and read the mail.

'I'll be over this afternoon. The case is finished, by the way.'

'That should be nice for the dancers.'

'For all of us.'

'Are you to continue *with those clients much longer?*'

'Only another week.'

* * * * * * * * * *

88

I did not get over to my office that afternoon, however, for just as I hung up the telephone Miss Ruger announced that the Executive Secretary of the Veterans' Committee awaited my pleasure.

'Show him in,' I said.

A thick burly veteran of the First World War rushed toward me; I slipped behind my desk, afraid of being tackled.

'The name's Fleer, Abner S. Fleer.'

'My name is . . .'

'I'll come straight to the point . . . no use mincing matters, is there? When you got something to say say it, that's what I say.'

'Shoot!' I said, showing that I could talk straight, too.

'We've been picketing your show, right?'

'Right.'

'I'll bet you'd like us *not* to picket your show, right?'

'Wrong.'

'Wrong?'

'It happens to be a very useful form of promotion, Mr. Frear.'

'Fleer. That remains to be seen. Veterans are staying away . . . I can tell you that.'

'Even without the veterans we are sold out not only for this season, but also on the road. We go to Chicago next week.'

'Only because you've been cashing in on the other immoral goings-on in your show.'

'You're referring to the murder?'

'I am indeed.'

'Well, a man killed his wife and now the man is dead of a heart attack . . . so that's all over.'

'We have reason to believe that your company is a hotbed of Reds and other undesirables.'

'What makes you think so?'

'Mister, we have spent close to a hundred thousand in the last year to root Reds and other perverts out of our way of life, in government, entertainment and the life of everyday . . . and we're doing it. We have reason to believe this man Wilbur is a party member.'

'If you can prove it why don't you get him indicted? Or whatever the procedure is.'

'Because these fellows are slippery. Oh, we've been tipped

off but that's a long way from getting a gander at his membership card.'

'Then why don't you wait until you *have* got it ... save a lot of bother.'

'There's a moral issue involved. It may take us years to track him down ... in the meantime he is corrupting our cherished ideals with his immoral dances. We want to put him out of commission right now and we're appealing to you as fellow Americans to help us.'

'But I'm not convinced he *is* a Communist and neither is Mr. Washburn.'

'We can show you reports from a dozen sources ...'

'Malicious gossip,' I said righteously.

'Are you trying to defend this radical?'

'I suppose I am. He is a great choreographer and I don't know anything about his politics and neither do you.'

'By the way, Mister, just what are *your* politics?'

'I am a Whig, Mr. Fleer. The last President I voted for was Chester A. Arthur.' On this mighty line, I got him out of the office, still shouting vengeance on all who attempted to sully our way of life.

I was pretty shaken by this interview with what was very likely one of the last perfect examples of Neanderthal man on the island of Manhattan. I went back into Mr. Washburn's office to get a drink ... I knew that he kept a bottle of very good brandy in a bottom drawer of his Napoleonic desk. Since he wasn't in, I took a mouthful right out of the bottle; then carefully, I put it back into the desk and idly glanced at the papers on his desk. One of them was a letter from Sylvia Armiger, the English ballerina ... a short note which I naturally read, saying that she would be unable to succeed Eglanova for the '52 season, that she was already under contract, but many thanks and so forth and so on.

The old bastard, I thought, amused by Washburn's duplicity. Even with Sutton gone he was still trying to replace Eglanova. I was less amused, though, when I noticed the date on the letter ... it was ten days old. It had been written *before* Ella Sutton's murder.

V

THE last night was a triumph. The box office reported that we had beaten all previous standing-room records for the Met and the audience was in a frantic mood, drowning out the music with almost continual applause for the stars who danced, I must say, with more skill than usual. If the audience was disappointed that the cable didn't break in *Eclipse*, they didn't show it for they called Jane back on stage seven times after the ballet. *Swan Lake* was magnificent in spite of several veterans who saw fit to heave a couple of firecrackers on to the stage . . . as well as a stink bomb which fortunately didn't go off.

Backstage, after the audience had left the theater, a great deal of vodka was stashed away by the Russian contingent . . . those members of the company born in Europe and their hangers-on . . . all singing and laughing and drinking vodka among the trunks and costumes. Eglanova was roaring drunk, weeping and laughing, her talk a mixture of Russian and English, all very confused.

Jane and I left early. Mr. Washburn caught us at the door and grandly gave me the next day off . . . after extending my contract another week. Jane, however, had to report at three-thirty the next day for rehearsal with Wilbur.

We spent the morning in bed, reading the newspapers and talking to people on the telephone, to dancers who were also spending this wonderful morning in bed, in various combinations. It was very cozy, like being part of a large family with, at the moment, no serious feuds to shatter the pleasant mood.

None of us could get over the fact that the investigation was finished, that Gleason was no longer a part of our lives.

'But,' as Jane said in her most professional voice over the telephone to one of the boy soloists, a Greek god with a voice like Bette Davis, 'where are we ever going to get another conductor as good as Miles?'

'I think Gold's working out fine,' I said, when she had hung up the telephone and was sitting cross-legged beside me on the bed, idly pinching my belly, trying to find a serious fold of flesh to complain about: she has always thought I do too little exercise . . . the reason, I always tell her, why I can eat everything and stay slim while she exercises, eats like a horse and has to watch her weight.

'You don't have to follow him,' she said irrelevantly, breathing deeply, rib-cage thrust forward, chin held high, breasts moving all of a piece, not quivering like jello the way most breasts do in this age of starch.

I grunted and shook her hand off my stomach as I read about our company, on page twenty-seven, in the *Globe*: 'Murdered Dancer's Husband Dead' . . . 'Suspected of Murder.' An interview with Gleason followed, on page twenty-eight, without photograph.

'Kind of nice *not* to be on the front page,' I said.

'Don't say that or you'll be thrown out of the Press Agents' guild or whatever it is that makes people like you the way they are.'

'The bitch goddess.'

'The what?'

'The ignoble concern with ephemeral reputation which has created people like me . . . professional criers, drumbeaters, trumpeters of brazen idols with feet of clay.'

'Oh, shut up. Does John Martin say anything in the *Times* about us?'

'He says that the Grand Saint Petersburg Ballet is leaving town next week for a five-month tour.'

She grabbed the *Times* away from me and read the column on 'Dance' with the desperate concentration of a ballerina hunting for a good notice.

'Certainly a plug for Eglanova,' she said at last, critically.

'Well, she's had a lot of them in her day.'

'Wouldn't it be wonderful if she retired of her own free will?' said my good-hearted girl.

'I don't see why. She'd be miserable. She doesn't want to teach. I think it's real fine the old woman can keep going like this . . . and still be a big draw all over the map.'

Jane scowled. 'It's so hard on the rest of us . . . I mean, it keeps everybody back.'

I snorted. 'Listen to her! A week ago you were one of those

lousy cygnets in *Swan Lake* pounding up and down the stage with three other girls in a Minsky routine and now you're thinking of the day when you'll succeed Eglanova.'

With one long liquid line as a certain ballet critic might have described it, Jane Garden dealt me a thunderous blow with the pillow. After a stiff fight, I subdued her at last . . . quite a trick considering she is a solid girl and, in spite of her lovely silklike skin, all muscle.

'It's not true!' she gasped, her hair like a net over the white sheets as I held her tight on her back.

'Delusions . . . that's what it is.'

'Everybody feels the same way. Ask any of the girls.'

'Vicious group . . . ambitious, untalented.'

'Oh!' And she twisted away from me and sat up in bed, breathing hard as she pushed her hair out of her face.

'It wouldn't surprise me one little bit if you knocked off Ella just to get her place in the company.'

Jane laughed mournfully. 'I don't need to tell you that our company works on the caste system. I was number seven ballerina before Ella died.'

'But now you're number two because you knew that if Ella was out of the picture I'd see to it you got her part.'

'Everything *has* worked out nicely,' said Jane, beaming.

'You have no conscience.'

'None at all. Especially now that the case is over.'

'Were you afraid of being caught?'

'Well, seriously, I didn't feel so good when poor Miles died.'

'Why?'

'Well, darling, I was there.'

'There?'

'I saw him about an hour before he died . . . I stopped off on my way to the party.'

'Good God!' I sat up in bed and looked at her . . . 'Did you tell Gleason that?'

'No, I didn't. I . . . I suppose I was afraid.'

'You little fool. . . .' I was alarmed. 'Don't you realize that he had that building watched, that Miles was being watched every minute of the day and night no matter where he was? Did you go in the front way?'

'Did I go in . . .? Of course I did. What do you think . . .'

'Then he knows that you were there and that you didn't

93

mention it when he questioned you. What do you think he'll make of that?'

'But . . . Miles did do it, didn't he? The case is closed?' she asked in a small voice. I sometimes think that dancers have less brains than the average vegetable.

'I don't know that he did and neither do the police. I have a hunch he didn't but I may be wrong. Even so, no matter what the papers say or Gleason says, those boys are still interested in what happened to Ella . . . and maybe to Miles, too.'

'I think you're exaggerating.' But she was scared.

'By the way, if I'm not being indiscreet, just what were you doing at Miles' apartment that night?'

'I had a message for him, from Magda.'

'Who paid a call on him later, after he was dead.'

'I know . . . but she wanted me to see him and tell him something. Her family was watching her like a hawk and she told me she wasn't able to get away and would I please go and see him.'

'This was before Don Ameche's invention of the telephone or the establishment of a national post office.'

'I wish you wouldn't try to be funny.'

'I couldn't be more serious.'

'Then act like it.'

'I am acting like it . . . God damn it . . .' We snarled at each other for several minutes; then she told me that Magda had not been able to leave her room for several days, that her family did not let her near the phone. Except for one stolen visit, Miles was not allowed to see her; as a matter of fact, the family had been reluctant to see even Jane.

'What did Magda want you to tell him?'

'What difference does it make now? . . . the whole thing's finished.'

'Come on . . . what did she want you to tell him?'

'It was about the child. She wanted to know if Miles would like her to have an abortion.'

'What did he say to that?'

'He said no, that they were going to get married as soon as the trial was over.'

'How was he when you saw him?'

'High as a kite . . . he didn't make much sense . . . he kept rambling about the new ballet . . . I mean about *Eclipse* and Mr. Washburn . . . he was angry at him. I don't know why.'

'Had Washburn been to see him?'

'No, not then.'

'How did you know he *did* see him that night?' I was like a district attorney, ready for the kill. But it didn't work.

'Because I saw Mr. Washburn outside in the street when I left and he asked me how Miles was, if he was high or not.'

'That was an awfully busy street that night, with half the company running in and out of Miles' apartment.'

'Oh, stop trying to be smart. You sound like a movie.'

'That may be,' I said somberly. 'Was Mr. Washburn upset when he saw you?'

'He was surprised; after all, we were both supposed to be at the party.'

'He didn't swear you to secrecy . . .'

'Oh, stop it, will you? I don't think it's funny.'

'I don't either. As a matter of fact it may be very serious . . . your having gone there without telling Gleason about it.'

'He didn't ask me. After all, I didn't lie to him.'

'What did he ask you?'

'Just a lot of questions . . . general things.'

It was no use; when Jane decides to be vague it is like collecting fragments of quicksilver from a broken thermometer to get a straight story out of her.

'You better go and tell Gleason what you told me.'

'I certainly won't now that everything's finished.'

'Then don't say I didn't warn you.'

At three o'clock I went to the office of the ballet and she went to rehearsal and neither of us was in a good mood. I was both angry and worried at what she had done. I wondered whether or not I should tell Gleason myself. For a number of reasons I decided not to. I *did* wonder if Mr. Washburn had told Gleason. This possibility had not occurred to me before; now, when I thought of it, my worry turned to alarm.

I found Mr. Washburn in his office playing with some silly putty which an admirer had given him; in case you haven't come across it, silly putty is a pink substance which, if rolled in a ball, will bounce better than rubber, which will shatter if you hit it with a hammer and which will stretch to an unbelievable length if you pull it . . . there is no point to silly putty and I took it as a serious sign that Mr. Washburn should now be stretching a long pink rope of it, like bubble gum, across his Napoleonic desk.

'I told you you could have the day off,' said my employer, unabashed, beginning to plait the substance. Had his mind snapped under the strain?

'I thought I'd drop by and take care of a few things. Toledo wants some photographs, so I thought . . .' I watched, fascinated, while Mr. Washburn made a hangman's noose.

'Wonderful house last night,' said Mr. Washburn. 'The best so far.'

'Good Press this morning.'

'Gratifying . . . gratifying. Did you ever see this stuff before?'

'Yes.'

'Wonderful idea . . . relaxes the nerves.' He rolled the putty into a ball and bounced it on the carpet where it sank deep; Mr. Washburn had to duck under his desk to retrieve it.

'By the way,' I asked, 'have you decided if you'll open the Chicago season with the new Wilbur ballet?'

'Mid-season . . . we'll do it our third week. I haven't picked the day yet.'

'Shall we do anything about Miles' funeral tomorrow?'

Mr. Washburn draped the silly putty over his upper lip like a moustache, only it looked more like some awful cancerous growth; he frowned. 'Better do nothing about it, Peter. The quicker this business is forgotten the better. Besides, it's going to be a family affair. A couple of aunts and a grandmother appeared on the scene, from Jersey, and they're in charge.'

'Are you going?'

Mr. Washburn shook his head and returned the silly putty to its egg-shaped plastic container. 'I don't think I will. I passed word on to the others that I thought it might be a good idea for them not to go either . . . papers would be sure to print a picture of Eglanova at the funeral, and give it space.'

'Then I won't go either.' I was relieved. I don't like funerals. Then I asked him, very casually, if he had said anything to the police about seeing Jane at Miles' apartment the night he died.

Mr. Washburn looked at me gravely. 'She was a very unwise young lady not to tell the police she was there.'

'Did *you* tell them?'

'No, I didn't. Which was unwise of me I suppose, but I have no intention of losing Garden just as she's begun to dance like a real ballerina. Under the circumstances I don't think the police are very much interested. After all, it's to their advantage to have the case finished.'

'I suppose you're right.'

'By the way, what did you tell that man from the Veterans' Committee yesterday?'

'I told him that it was up to them to prove Wilbur was a Communist.'

Mr. Washburn chuckled. 'You will be happy to know that you have been accused of being a Communist-sympathizer, a party-liner, a fellow-traveller and a degenerate by one Abner Fleer . . . have you got anything to say in your defense?'

'Nothing at all . . . except that I was driven into the hands of the enemy by Mr. Fleer and his kind in the days of my youth; even before my America First button had begun to tarnish, I found myself disenchanted with the keepers of the flame.'

'I sympathize with you. The charges against Wilbur are getting serious, though. The columnists are beginning to take up the question, and, frankly, I'm worried about Chicago. It's not like New York. The Veterans' Committee is a joke here but out there it carries a lot of weight and we may be in trouble if they decide to blackball us.'

'What can we do?'

'I wish I knew.'

'Couldn't we take an ad and say that he's already been cleared twice?'

'We'll have to do something like that. Think about it, anyway. That's our big assignment for the next week . . . getting Mr. Wilbur, and us, off the hook.'

'I'll think of something,' I said with the same air of quiet confidence which has made a fortune for any number of movie actors, con-men and politicians.

Eglanova, in a summer dress and a set of sables (the day was hot but she wouldn't be Eglanova without sable), swept into the office. We both rose and Mr. Washburn leaned across the desk and kissed her hand.

'Such wonderful last night!' she exclaimed, glowing with pleasure. 'Such applause! Such loyalty! I weep to remember it.'

But her narrow mascaraed eyes were dry, the lashes as artfully curled as ever.

'Darling Anna! You are the *prima* of our time . . . the ultimate.'

'Such nice thing to say, Ivan. Of course last night I *tried*. That makes difference. But those *awful* people!' She scowled, looking like Attila the Hun or maybe Genghis Khan contemplating traitors. 'Who *are* these people anyway? Who are people who throw things when Eglanova dances? Ivan, you must do something.'

'They weren't throwing things at you, Anna. They were throwing them at Wilbur.'

'Even so they hit *me* when I dance Swan Queen. If they don't like Jed why don't they throw things during *Eclipse?*'

Mr. Washburn laughed. 'I expect they intended to but they got their signals mixed. In any case, we won't have trouble with them in Chicago . . . rest assured.' Eglanova did not look as though she were resting assured but she changed the subject.

'Dear Peter,' she said, turning to me and smiling a dazzling smile, 'I must thank you for not telling police about those big scissors. It was sweet of you . . . very brave. I thank you.' And she patted my arm.

'I told her,' said Mr. Washburn. 'I told her that you didn't want to incriminate her.'

I mumbled something graceful and incoherent.

'So strange,' sighed Eglanova. 'Why would Miles want to put scissors in my room? *I* who am last person to harm fellow artist.'

Both Mr. Washburn and I expressed wonder at the murderer's intention; then, aware that some ballet plot was afoot, I excused myself. I was sure, even then, that Mr. Washburn had told the police about having seen Jane at Miles' apartment.

2

Jane and I were very cool with one another that evening and even cooler the next morning when we got up early, at ten o'clock, and made breakfast. She was angry at my having scolded her and I was alarmed at her bad sense; the fact that the night had passed without love-making didn't put me in a very good mood either.

It wasn't until we had finished a pot of coffee between us, that I told her what Mr. Washburn had said.

'Well, there wasn't any reason for him to say I was there.' She looked sulky and she wore her dressing gown which was a bad sign . . . usually neither of us wears any clothes around the apartment.

'Except that he could get into trouble, too, for not mentioning it . . . but I've got a hunch he *did* tell them . . . if only because they know already.'

'I think you're making an awful fuss about nothing . . . that's what I think,' said Jane, massaging her calves.

'How was the rehearsal?'

'Tough.' She sighed. 'It isn't like a rehearsal with Alyosha . . . I'll say that. Wilbur screams at you and half the time I think he makes up the ballet as he goes along.'

'I wonder if it'll be any good?'

'I suppose so. They say this is the way he always works.'

'He wasn't like this during *Eclipse*, was he?'

'He was pretty noisy . . . of course I wasn't there too much of the time. He worked mainly with the principals . . . especially Louis.'

'How's the big affair coming?'

'Not so well . . . I don't think Louis likes him very much.'

'But he likes Louis?'

'Madly. You should see the way he looks at him, like a spaniel or something.'

The telephone rang. Jane answered it. She said 'yes' several times then she said, 'Come right over.' And hung up.

'Who was that?'

'Magda. She's given up her apartment and she's going to move in here.'

'I see.' I turned to ice, thinking of my own lonely apartment downtown.

'I thought I'd let her stay on here after we go to Chicago. She'll look after the apartment and everything.'

'And for the next week?'

'Well, I mean it's only a week . . .'

'And I can go home?'

'But think of all she's gone through . . . not a friend in the world except me. As a matter of fact, she may be pretty sick starting tomorrow.'

'Why?'

'She's found a doctor who'll . . . you know . . . fix her, take care of the baby.'

'What about her family?'

'They've gone back to Boston, thank God.'

For a number of reasons, none charitable, I thought it best not to complain. With the air of a martyr surveying the flames, I packed my suitcase while Jane telephoned all her friends to discuss Magda, the ballet, Jed Wilbur and the doings of rival companies.

We were both dressed and ready to leave when Magda appeared, looking dumpy in a linen suit and carrying a suitcase. The two girls embraced tenderly.

'I hope I'm not being too awful ... I mean moving in like this,' said Magda, looking at me with red-rimmed eyes. She had obviously been weeping steadily for over a week now. I never felt more uncompassionate toward anyone in my life, at that moment anyway.

'Of course not,' I said, with an attempt at cheeriness. 'I think it's wonderful ... now that your family's gone.'

'We were just going to rehearsal,' said Jane. 'Why don't you make yourself at home. I'll be back at five.'

'Do you think they'd mind if I went too? I'd like to sit and watch awhile ... see what the new ballet's like.' She sounded very wistful. 'I can get my other bags later.'

'That's a fine idea,' said Jane who seemed more pleased with this new arrangement than she had any reason to be. So I grabbed the suitcase, bade the ladies farewell and took a cab for my Ninth Street apartment. Then, after a visit with Miss Flynn at my own office, I walked to the studio.

The Grand Saint Petersburg Ballet operates a school over in Hell's Kitchen, on the West Side. They occupy the fifth floor of a terrible old building which should have been condemned long ago. Their section, however, has been done up handsomely, very modern, and they have four classrooms as well as a large studio which is often used for rehearsal, sparing Mr. Washburn the unnecessary expense of hiring halls which he occasionally has to do during the season.

I arrived at about three-thirty and visited some of the classes before I went to the room where Jed Wilbur was creating like mad with Jane and most of the company.

There was a very chic-looking reception hall where the dancers often sit about in tights waiting for their hour in class, a long hall decorated with mobiles and paintings of dancers, with a desk at one end where Madame Aloin, formerly of the Paris

Opera, sits in splendor and receives visitors and incoming telephone calls.

I said good afternoon to Madame Aloin who gave me a stately nod; then I wandered into the nearest classroom. Here a number of dismal tiny tots were being run through a set of exercises by a bored, overweight dancer who had once been celebrated before his thyroid had begun malfunctioning. The mothers, a row of somber ladies, grey and determined, glared at me as the piano plunked one two one two. I shut the door.

The next two classrooms were more interesting: lovely blond girls in black tights practising intricate variations with a group of muscle-bound cissies. Somewhat aroused, *wanting* to be aroused since I was angry at Jane, at the celibacy she had arranged for me, I went to the fourth classroom which was empty, a cube of a room, like the rest, with mirrors at one end and a waist-high bar at the other end where the dancers did exercises, and tall windows which went almost to the floor. In one corner of this room is a door which opens into the rehearsal hall, a sneak entrance often used by the stars when they want to get out quickly, when they see the bores, the balletomanes, waiting for them at the main door.

The rehearsal looked like a panic. Most of the *corps de ballet* was there, in tights and T-shirts, drenched with sweat, as the piano banged out a phrase of Poulenc, over and over, while Wilbur shouted excitedly at them, his thin grey hair on end and his face flushed.

'Lift with the music! Lift with the music . . . it's not that difficult. Listen . . . there is your phrase. Lift the girls on the second beat, start it then, finish on the fourth. Da da dum dada . . . hear? Da da *lift* . : . da da *lift!* Now try it again.'

I sat down on the long hard bench by the door and watched the *corps de ballet* go through its paces. They all looked tired and wretched in the heat. I was glad I wasn't a dancer. Jane seemed worried as she did her solo in front of the company who were, in the meantime, doing a complicated movement behind her. Louis, who was not in this particular part, came ambling over to me with his usual grin. 'Hi, Baby . . . long time no see.' For some reason, Louis, when he learned English, absorbed a great deal of Nineteen-twenty slang which sounds very funny coming from him, with his French accent and all. He sat down beside me, his knee shoved hard against mine. I moved away.

'You want to go up to Harlem with me tonight? I got a couple cute numbers there . . . oh, you like them fine.'

'I got enough where I am, Honey,' I said, falling into his way of talking.

'That's too bad. We could have a swell time, you and me . . . up in Harlem.'

'Not my idea of a swell time.'

'What sort of boy are you? American boys all like . . .' and he made an obscene gesture. I glanced around nervously but nobody was watching us . . . the music covered our voices and Wilbur was giving the dancers hell.

'I guess I'm un-American,' I said.

'Maybe you like real young boys . . . maybe I'm too old for you.'

'Louis, you're my idea of heaven . . . honest to God you are, but I'd feel selfish having you all to myself when the fellows in the company need you so much more than I do. Why I wouldn't even know how to begin to appreciate you.'

'I teach you in one plenty fast lesson.' And I moved away as that sinewy leg slammed against mine. Then Wilbur saw his love and with a look of real alarm said, 'Louis! That's your cue.' And our hero bounded to his feet and joined Wilbur and Jane in the center of the room. '*Adagio!*' shouted Wilbur to the pianist; the boys and girls relaxed, wilted in decorative attitudes against the bar, talking to each other in low voices while Louis and Jane did their *pas de deux*.

I got up and stretched my legs. Magda came into the hall and smiled wanly at me.

'How is it going?' she asked.

'Damned if I can tell. Looks like a riot from where I'm sitting.'

'It usually works out,' she said vaguely, sitting down. 'How does Jane look?'

'Worried,' I said, flatly; I was angry with Miss Garden.

'Such a responsibility, having a new ballet being made for you.'

'And a few other people.'

Eglanova and Alyosha entered the room, like an old king and queen come to watch the heirs-apparent at play. They nodded regally to Wilbur and the company and then they sat down on the bench, very straight. I joined them.

I chatted with Alyosha while Eglanova and Magda watched Wilbur at work.

'Such great confusion,' said Alyosha. 'No one can tell what it is. I hope he is nearly done, though.'

'Why?'

'He must go to Washington on Wednesday,' Alyosha did not bother to disguise his pleasure.

'To be investigated?'

'Exactly . . . very secret hearing, but I found out . . . now it is not so secret!' Alyosha laughed.

'Does Wilbur know?'

'I'm sure he does. So I hope the ballet will be ready in case he doesn't come back from Washington for a few days.' Or years, I could hear our *regisseur* say to himself. Old Alyosha was, I knew, afraid that he would be retired one of these days, be replaced by one of the bright young men, like Jed Wilbur.

'Looks like the veterans have carried the day,' I said.

'Pretty girl!' said Eglanova as Jane did some glittering *chassé* turns into Louis' arms.

'In ten years she will be ready to take your place,' said Alyosha gallantly.

'Dear friend!' said our star, her eyes black slits as she watched Jane do her stuff.

Then the door to the hall opened and Mr. Washburn peered in at us; he gestured for me to join him. I slipped out of the hall and joined him in the reception room.

'More trouble,' he said with a sigh.

'About the hearings in Washington?'

'Exactly. I think it'll be in all the papers tomorrow. I was trying to hush it up but now it's too late. The F.B.I. is mixed up in the case.'

'He's not guilty, is he?'

'I don't think so. I don't think that they have anything important. They only want to question him . . . but that's enough to get all the witch-hunters in this town against us. Not to mention Chicago.'

'What can we do?'

'Make it appear that he's testifying of his own free will . . . which I suppose he is, in a way. We'll try and make a big thing of his turning informer . . . you know what I mean: ex-liberal telling what he knows about Communism in the theater.'

'Seems kind of sick-making.'

'So what? We've got a long tour ahead of us and I've tied up a good deal of money in Wilbur.' You and Alma Edderdale and twenty other patrons, I thought.

'Have you talked it over with Wilbur?'

'Oh yes . . . just before rehearsal this afternoon. He's going to follow the same line. He doesn't want trouble . . . especially if he's innocent, and signed to do the new Hayes and Marks musical in the fall . . .' he added irrelevantly.

'What do you want me to do then? Get in touch with the papers directly? Or work through the columnists?'

'Get to the papers directly; but first you'll have to handle Elmer Bush. He's on his way over to look around, he says, but of course he's going to try and get some kind of exclusive out of Jed or me. Now I'm going to keep out of sight and I'm going to keep Jed away from Bush, if possible. Your job is to head him off . . . even if you have to hint that Jed has got some wild revelations for the committee in Washington.'

'I'll do what I can,' I said, like the Spartan youth with the fox at his vitals.

'Good fellow,' said Mr. Washburn, hurrying down the hall to the classroom of tiny tots where he intended, obviously, to hide out until Elmer Bush, a symphony in blue: shirt, suit, socks and tie, appeared in our reception hall, causing a bit of a stir among the dancers who were sitting on the benches waiting to go into class . . . it was five minutes to the hour.

'Why hello there,' said Mr. Bush, flashing that television smile of his, the dentures superbly wrought and fitted. 'Washburn or Wilbur around? . . . old friend of mine, Ivan Washburn.' In spite of his fame and power he still had the reporter's nervous habit of trying a little too hard to establish friendship with persons in high and interesting places, for the moment interesting, for the moment news.

'They aren't here right now, Mr. Bush . . . is there anything I can do for you?'

'Call me Elmer,' said the great man mechanically, taking in the room with a reporter's eyes, a lecher's eye too, for his gaze paused longer than necessary over one of the girls, a slim brown-haired number with a T-shirt. 'Nice place you people have here. Terrible neighborhood, though. Been fighting for years now to

104

get it cleaned up. Made absolutely no headway. When do you expect Wilbur?'

It took me a moment to separate the question from what had promised to be a thoughtful Elmer Bush report of city-planning. 'Well, you know he's pretty busy with that new ballet.'

'They're rehearsing it here.'

Since this wasn't a question, but a statement, I had to agree. 'But nobody's allowed in the studio while he's working. He's very difficult.'

'We'll see how difficult he is when that committee gets through with him in Washington.'

'How did you know about that . . . Elmer?' I asked, very folksy, my eyes round with admiration.

'Never ask an old reporter to tell his sources,' chuckled Bush, pleased with the effect he thought he was making.

'Why, *I* only heard about it an hour ago.'

'That so? Then tell me this . . . how do you people plan to get your big wheel off the spot?'

'Well, for one thing we happen to know he's not a Communist and for another thing he's going to tell all he knows about the Reds in the theater.'

'It's a closed hearing, too,' said Bush thoughtfully. 'Got any idea about some of the names he's going to mention?'

'Nobody very big,' I invented glibly. 'A few of the old North American Ballet Company people, that's about all.'

'You've been having a busy time, haven't you, Peter,' said Bush, suddenly focusing his attention on me for the first time in our long if superficial acquaintanceship.

'I'll say.'

'They really wind that Sutton case up?'

'I think so . . . don't you?'

'Haven't heard anything to the contrary . . . worked out very neatly, from the police's point of view . . . no trial, no expense for the stage . . . perfect case.' While we talked I kept trying to edge him into the empty classroom before the hour struck, before four o'clock when Wilbur would take a break, on the dot, because that's a company rule even the most temperamental choreographers have to obey. But Mr. Bush wouldn't budge: the secret perhaps of his success. At four o'clock the door to the studio opened and thirty tired and messy dancers came charging out, heading for the dressing rooms, the drinking fountain, the telephone . . . I have a theory that dancers, next to hostesses, spend more time telephoning than any other single group in America.

Elmer Bush kept on talking but his eyes looked like they were on swivels, like the chameleon who can see in all directions. At first he couldn't spot anybody; then I waved to Jane who was standing by the door to the empty classroom, adjusting the ribbon to one of her toeshoes. It was five after four. She waved above the noisy crowd of dancers, parents and tiny tots (all the classes let out on the hour) and, breathless, came to us through a sea of sweating dancers.

'This is the young ballerina in *Eclipse*, Mr. Bush . . . Jane Garden.'

They shook hands and Jane was pretty enough to distract Bush's attention long enough for Mr. Washburn to sneak past us, in the shadow of the corpulent teacher of dance with whom he pretended to talk. Before he got to the door, however, the first policeman had arrived.

3

It took them four hours to question the *corps de ballet*, parents, even the tiny tots, most of whom were whining loudly at this unexpected turn of events. But by the time Gleason had arrived, only the principals were left, all seated glumly in the studio, on that hard bench.

The body of Magda had been taken immediately to the morgue and though none of us had seen it the rumor was that she had been pretty badly smashed by her fall from the window of the classroom adjoining the rehearsal studio.

A policeman stood in the door of the studio, watching us as though we were wild animals. Inspector Gleason did not present himself to us upon arrival; we heard his full-throated Irish voice, however, as he had a desk set up for himself in the empty classroom. Here he received us, one by one.

We talked very little during those hours. Mr. Washburn, with remarkable presence of mind, had summoned his lawyer who waited now with a brief case full of writs calculated to circumvent any and every vagary of justice.

Eglanova, after one brilliant outburst of Imperial Moscow

anger, had settled down to a quiet chat with Alyosha, in Russian. Alyosha was more nervous; he continually screwed and unscrewed his monocle, wiping it with a silk handkerchief. Jane, who sat beside me, wept a little and I comforted her. Wilbur, after a display of Dubuque, Iowa, temperament, settled down for a long tense quarrel with Louis, a quarrel which had nothing to do with Magda. For some reason Madame Aloin had been placed under suspicion as well as the pianist, a worm-white youth who acted exactly the way you would suppose a murderer at bay to act. Mr. Washburn was not with us long, since he was the first witness to be called. I might add that Elmer Bush had contrived to remain with us in the studio, after first phoning his numerous staff: this was one exclusive he was sure of . . . television star or not he was the same Elmer Bush who, twenty years ago, was the best crime reporter in the country. He chatted with everyone now . . . first with one; then with another, conducting a suave investigation which I swear, was a good deal brighter than the one the taxpayer's burden was conducting in the next room.

'Come on, baby,' I whispered to Jane, my arm around her. 'Don't take it so hard. It's just one of those things . . .' I whispered stupidly, soothingly, because after a while she stopped and dried her eyes with a crumpled piece of Kleenex.

'I can't believe it,' she said, shaking her head. 'Not Magda . . . not like that.'

'Tell them everything, Jane . . . everything. This is serious. Tell them about your being at Miles' place.'

'Poor Magda . . .'

'You'll do that, won't you?'

'What? Do what?' I told her again and she looked surprised. 'But what's that got to do with Magda?'

'It may have everything to do with her, with all of us. Promise you'll tell Gleason the whole story.'

'If you think I ought to.'

'I do. I'm sure all three of these things are connected.'

'So am I,' said Jane, unexpectedly.

I was surprised . . . she had always been very unrealistic about the trouble . . . almost as bad as Mr. Washburn and his 'accident' theories. I asked her why she had changed her mind.

'Something Magda said today . . . something about Miles . . . I don't remember exactly what it was but she . . . I think she knew who killed Ella. I think Miles must have known all along and told her that day when he went to see her, when she was sick and her family happened to be out.'

'She—didn't tell you who it was?'

'Do you think I would be sitting here like this scared to death if she had? I'd be right in there with that policeman, telling him I wanted somebody arrested before . . . before this happens again.' She shuddered suddenly and I felt cold myself. I looked about the room wildly, wondering who it was. Which of these people was a murderer? Or had someone who wasn't even here killed Ella and Magda, a maniac in the *corps de ballet* . . . ?

'I wonder just what happened?' I asked, changing the subject.

'I know,' said Elmer Bush smoothly; he had sat down next to me without my knowing it . . . what a break this was for him: witness, or near-witness to a murder, a flashy, glamorous murder. He could hardly keep a straight face, hardly disguise his delight at what had happened. 'A terrible tragedy,' he said in a low voice, the one used to announce the death of forty passengers on a transatlantic airliner, or corruption in Washington.

'How did it happen?'

'She was pushed through the window . . . one minute after four o'clock,' said Elmer and the tip of his tongue, quick as a lizard's, moistened his lips.

'By party or parties unknown,' I said.

'Exactly. Her purse was found on the floor; her body on the sidewalk seven stories below.'

'The purse . . .'

He finished my sentence: 'Had been searched. Its contents were scattered over the floor. Whoever did it must've grabbed the purse away from her and then, quick as a flash, shoved her through the window and searched the handbag for something . . .'

'Robbery?' suggested Jane weakly.

We both ignored her. 'I wonder what they were looking for?'

'When we know that,' said Elmer slowly, in his best doom voice, 'we will know who killed Ella and Miles Sutton.'

I remember hoping at the time that the three murders were totally unconnected, just to prove this unctuous vulture wrong.

'Tell me,' said Elmer gently, turning to Jane, 'did she seem at all odd to you when you went into that room together?'

'Sweet Jesus!' I cried softly, turning to Jane. 'You weren't with her, were you? You weren't there, too?'

'Always on the spot,' said Jane with a faint attempt at lightness.

'Does Gleason know this?'

'I plan to tell him . . . honest I will, Peter.'

'He knows anyway,' said omniscient Elmer. 'Did she say something which might throw any light on what happened?'

'No, she didn't.'

'Why did you go in there with her?'

'Now listen, Bush,' I snapped, 'stop playing Mr. District Attorney. She's gone through enough.'

'That's all right, Peter.' She rallied a bit. 'Magda wasn't feeling well. She's going . . . she *was* going to have a baby and she suddenly felt sick. I took her in there when the rehearsal was over . . . it was the only place on the floor where she wouldn't be crowded. Then I left her and talked to you . . . Maybe she fell. She could have, you know. Those windows . . . well, look over there: they almost go down to the floor.'

'Fell? After first emptying her purse over the studio floor?' Elmer shook his head. 'Somebody shoved her. Was there anybody else in the room?'

Jane shook her head wearily. 'I said it was empty.'

'Anybody could have gone in there,' said Elmer Bush, staring at the door at the far end of the room, behind which we could hear the distant rumble of Gleason's voice as he questioned Mr. Washburn.

The interviews went fairly fast. Eglanova, Alyosha, Wilbur, Louis, Madame Aloin, the pianist, Jane, myself. By the time my turn came around, it was already dark outside and the overhead fluorescent lights had been turned on, a ghastly blue light, reflected by tall mirrors.

The first thing I noticed was the window. For some reason I had supposed that it had been open when she fell out. It hadn't occurred to me that she would have been pushed through a pane of glass . . . which is what had happened.

Gleason looked much as ever and I noticed the same pale secretary was on hand taking notes; otherwise, the room was empty . . . no police, no furniture, no rifled handbag.

We got through the preliminaries quickly. I could see that he was not very much interested in me . . . possibly because Elmer had already told him that I was with him in the hall when the murder took place . . . what was that wonderful word they use to describe someone being pushed through a window: defenestration?

He wanted to know what, if anything, Madga had said to me that morning.

'She didn't talk much to me . . . I know she told Jane about her abortion. She was going to have it tomorrow; that was her plan.'

'In the meantime she was going to live with Miss Garden?'

'That's right.'

'Ordinarily you live in Miss Garden's apartment?'

I blushed. 'For the last week or so,' I said. 'Do you plan to book me for lewdness?'

Gleason showed his teeth in a friendly snarl. 'This is homicide, Sargeant, not the vice squad.' He enjoyed saying my last name; he made it sound like a police rank, a subordinate rank. 'We have reason to think the deaths of Ella Sutton and Magda Foote were the work of the same person.'

'I think so, too.'

'Why?'

'Because a few days ago at the theater, Magda told us, Jane and me, that she knew Miles was innocent and that he knew who had killed Ella. I asked her then if he'd told her and she said no he hadn't but I thought she was lying . . . I'm positive she was lying. I'll bet anything Magda knew.'

'If she knew why didn't she come to us?'

'I don't know why. For one thing, she probably didn't care whether you ever caught Ella's murderer or not . . . after all she hated Ella and Miles' death was an accident, wasn't it?'

'As far as we know. Why wouldn't Miles Sutton have told us who killed Ella when he knew he was our number one suspect, that we were going to arrest him the second we could break his alibi . . . and we broke it, finally.'

'According to Magda, he wasn't going to say anything until the trial . . . or until you arrested him. I think he hoped you wouldn't be able to pin it on anybody.'

'That wasn't very realistic.'

'I'd hardly call a man as far gone on drugs as Miles realistic . . . remember that whoever killed Ella was doing him a service. He wouldn't turn the murderer in . . . unless it was to save his own neck.'

Gleason asked me some more questions, about members of the company, about Magda, pointless questions, or so they seemed to me . . . and probably were in fact because it was quite obvious that the police were completely at sea. I was then told to come back the next day for questioning, to stay in New York City at an address where I could be reached at a moment's notice . . . I gave him Jane's address.

She was waiting for me in the reception hall. Everyone had gone except Louis and herself and Wilbur. Louis had apparently just come from the shower room for his hair was gleaming with water, the celebrated black curls damp and straggly. Jane was also in her street clothes, looking very pale, her face not made up. Wilbur was talking excitedly, 'As if I didn't have enough trouble without all this. A major investigation hanging over my head . . . I was supposed to go to Washington tomorrow . . . and a half-finished ballet and now one of those god-damned murder investigations this company seems to specialize in. I wish to hell I'd stayed in musical comedy. Nothing like this ever happened there.'

'Shows we were just waiting for you, Jed,' said Louis amiably. 'It was all Mr. Washburn's idea to knock you off so Alyosha would remain the greatest living choreographer.'

'Much help you've been through all this,' said Jed spitefully. Jane and I got out before the lovers quarreled.

We both took it for granted that I was not going to go to my place after what happened. Jane was terrified at the thought of being alone.

'I'm sure it's a lunatic,' she said, when we were back at the apartment, eating cold cuts and drinking beer from the near-by delicatessen. 'How do we know he isn't going to murder everybody in the company while the police sit by and let him kill us, one by one?'

'Come on, kid,' I said, as calmly as possible. 'Get a grip on yourself. Your old buddy is right here with you.'

'I'm still frightened,' she said, chewing a piece of liverwurst thoughtfully. 'Not just of the murderer either.'

'The police?'

She nodded.

'Did you tell Gleason about having been at Miles' apartment?'

'I told him everything.'

'Then you have nothing to fear,' I said heartily, beginning to slip out of my clothes.

'Pull the shade down,' said Jane.

'You *are* jumpy.' As a rule we never put the shade down or put the lights out either. But I went over to the window and drew the curtains; they stuck a little and by the time I had pulled them together I had seen the plainclothes man across the street, watching the apartment.

I remember thinking how unusual it was to be making love to a girl who was thought by some to have murdered two, maybe three people.

VI

MEDICAL examination, inquest, more questioning . . . it promised to be a long day. When I was not participating in the official rites of investigation, conducted as solemnly as a church service by Gleason, I was at the office holding Mr. Washburn's hand and battling some thirty newsmen who had appeared at nine o'clock in the morning (proving we were news) and stayed in the anteroom chatting with our duo-typists most of the day, complaining about the meager handouts they got from me. The police were saying nothing and I had silenced the members of our company. Even so there were a dozen wild theories in the air and the editorial in the afternoon *Globe* demanded that the murderer be instantly produced . . . if not, the *Globe* suggested balefully, there might be some changes made in the office of the Commissioner.

I was almost afraid to read the columns that afternoon. The news stories were all right: they just reported the facts, which were few . . . Third Murder in Ballet Mystery. But the columnists, in their own libelous way, were hinting pretty strongly that someone highly placed in the ballet world, in our company, had done the three murders. Needless to say, in spite of the official theory, everyone was convinced that there was a connection between the deaths of Miles and Ella and Magda. The *Globe* had the inside story. Beloved Elmer Bush had seen to that. His column made the front page . . . an exclusive report by An Eyewitness.

'Little did I think, as I talked with the beauteous Magda, that a few moments later she would lie broken and alone in the street below. She must have known even then what fate had in store for her. There was something other-worldly in her manner, a remoteness, a true serenity. I think she wanted to join her friend Miles Sutton in a better world, to be as one with the father of her unborn child. Yet as we stood talking to one another in that busy rehearsal studio, a murderer was watching

113

us, plotting her destruction. Did she know his (or her?) identity? Yes, I have reason to believe she did . . .'

'I don't want to hear any more,' said Mr. Washburn, draining his third shot of brandy.

'It's more of the same,' I said, putting the paper down on the floor, to join the pile by my chair. We were in his office. One of the duo-typists had brought us sandwiches for lunch and the newsmen had momentarily deserted us. We were taking no calls and reading no mail.

'I wonder if we shouldn't take that South American tour . . . we could leave next week . . . well, in two weeks' time anyway. First Guatemala City then Panama, Bogotá, Rio, Buenos Aires . . .' Naming these remote places seemed to soothe my employer who sat now sniffing his empty brandy glass, his eyes bloodshot and glazed.

'I'm afraid the police wouldn't let us go,' I said gently.

He pulled himself together with a visible effort. 'You take over,' he said, as though I hadn't been in charge all along, since nine anyway. 'I'm going down to City Hall. After that, I'll be at the studio in case you want me.'

'The rehearsals still going on?'

'Oh yes. Gleason was very decent about that. In fact, he's moved into one of the classrooms . . . the one where . . .' He stopped. 'I suppose he wants to be on the scene.'

'Try and stop them,' I said, as Mr. Washburn placed his panama squarely on the center of his long head, the brim parallel to the floor.

'Stop who?'

'The police . . . when you see them. I think they're going to make an arrest.'

'What makes you think so?'

'First, because I've read the papers today. They want an arrest. And, second, because Jane is being watched by the police.'

'I'm sure they don't suspect her.'

'It's a toss-up, Mr. Washburn, between her and Eglanova.'

He shuddered. 'Don't say that. Don't even think it.'

'I'm perfectly willing not to think it but some of these columnists won't be so obliging. They've done everything except name names. "Jealous ballerina" . . . that's their line, and that could mean only one of two people.'

'Let's wait until we come to this bridge,' said Mr. Washburn, with the air of a man ready to fall into a river. Then he left the office.

But I couldn't wait. I wasn't really worried about Jane. She was obviously innocent and if they indicted her they wouldn't be able to convict. I was confident of that. But even if justice prevailed she would be marked all her life as the girl who had been accused of a murder. I can still remember what happened to a certain musical comedy star back in the Thirties.

I sat at Mr. Washburn's desk for several minutes, more worried than I'd ever been in my life. Idly, with a pencil stub, I began to write names: Eglanova, Wilbur, Alyosha, Washburn, Louis . . . I stopped; then I wrote Jane's name at the bottom. I made a box around it, carefully, an elaborate doodle, like a wall protecting her. I was confident that one of those six had been responsible for the murders. But which one? I had to admit to myself that for all I cared the murderer could go free. The Suttons and Magda meant nothing to me; if someone disliked them or feared them enough to want to kill them, well, that was hardly my business. A callous way of looking at things but you must remember that I liked the suspects, most of them anyway, and I wished them no harm . . . I'm not a crusader or a reformer and I have no passion for justice: not the crazy way the world is now at least. Official murder, private murder . . . what's the difference? Not much, except when you're involved yourself or someone you care about is. The more I thought about it the madder I got.

I was very grim when I wrote 'Why?' at the top of the page; then, next to it, I wrote 'How?' Just trying to be methodical made everything seem much better. At least it was all in front of me . . . like a crossword puzzle, or a double acrostic. If I could only fill in the blanks under each column I might be able to figure it out without leaving my desk . . . as you see, I have that happy faith in logic which only a liberal arts education can give.

Eglanova. Why? Well, she didn't want to retire. She knew that Mr. Washburn could not get another ballerina with her pull at the box office for at least a year . . . except Ella Sutton. That was motive enough for someone of Eglanova's dedication. As for Miles and Magda, I was convinced that their deaths were connected with Ella's, that they had been killed because they knew who the murderer was . . . which took care of the 'Why?'

of their deaths. So the only important motive was the original one: who wanted to kill Ella Sutton; who had the strongest *known* motive? The answer was Eglanova. When could she have done the murders? Presuming that Miles had been murdered in some mysterious way. Well, she was at the theater from dress rehearsal to performance, almost continuously. She could have cut the cable any time. And Miles? She was at the party Alma Edderdale gave and she could have left at any time, gone to his apartment and climbed the fire escape without being seen by the police. But even as I checked her in, made it possible for her to have visited Miles, I felt a certain misgiving: it was not in character. Anna Eglanova might in a rage eliminate a rival, but I could hardly see the great ballerina skulking up a fire escape in the middle of the night. Of course everything is possible. As for Magda . . . well, any of my six suspects could have pushed her out of that window. There was such confusion when the rehearsal broke up that someone could have followed Magda into the classroom, grabbed the purse, shoved her out the window and slipped back into the studio, all undetected.

Sadly, I crossed out 'How?' at the top of the page. It wouldn't work, or rather it worked too well: no one had an alibi. Each time the doughty six had been in the same place at more or less the same time and all had equal opportunity to commit the murders. So, instead of 'How?' I wrote a large question mark over the column next to 'Why?' Here I recorded the mysteries.

Opposite Eglanova's name I wrote 'Shears'. If she had sliced the cable, why did she leave the shears in her own dressing room? That was a problem which I left unsolved as I moved on to the next name on the list.

Wilbur. Why? God knows. He didn't get on with Sutton but obviously if he hated her, for some reason as yet unknown, he would hardly have come to work in the same company with her, create a whole new ballet around her. Was he jealous of her? No. He didn't like women to begin with; nor did their love interests overlap. Professional jealousy? None that I could see. Something in the past, perhaps? Mysteries? Why did he quarrel with Ella the afternoon of the day she was killed?

Alyosha. Why? Love for Eglanova and hatred of Ella his ex-mistress. That was clear-cut, a perfect crime of passion. He had been married to Eglanova, left her for Ella who had deserted him; then he went back to Eglanova, as official slave and acolyte,

116

and now, seeing that Eglanova was soon to be succeeded by Sutton, he lost his head and removed Ella from this vale of tears. Mysteries? Why would he put the shears in Eglanova's dressing room, implicating her if he'd done the murder for love of her? My head began to ache. Those god-damned shears . . . they made a mess of every theory. Then a new idea occurred to me. Suppose the person who had done the murder had put the shears some place else and then another villain had, for malicious reasons, put them in Eglanova's room from which I moved them again . . . button button who's got the button?

Washburn. Why? Well, he is the most devious man alive. For all I know he may have wanted to get rid of both Sutton and Eglanova, and he saw this as a perfect way to take care of them. Among the mysteries was the fact of that letter I found from Armiger, the English ballerina. Why had Mr. Washburn wanted to engage a big star when the succession had already been arranged, when it had been all but announced that Sutton was to succeed Eglanova for the next season? And what was Mr. Washburn really up to at Miles' apartment that night?

Louis. Why? I could think of no reason. There was an old rumor in the company that Ella fancied him but since he was so obviously interested in the other side he could hardly have been disturbed by her love for him, presuming that glacier had ever experienced such a tender emotion. I made a note to ask Louis about Ella; it was possible that he had some unsuspected slant on her character. More and more I was convinced that her character would provide the clue to the puzzle.

Jane? Well, despite the mysterious visit to Miles and her incriminating presence in the classroom with Magda, she had no motive. She was not in line to succeed Sutton even though she was the understudy in *Eclipse*. She had no professional reason for wanting Ella out of the way and after living a while with her, I was fairly sure she had no private reason as well; their private lives had never touched, as far as I knew.

Gloomily, I studied the page, awaiting revelation. None came. The thought that my hypothesis might be wrong was chilling. I was going on the theory that X had killed Ella, that Miles had found out and was on the point of revealing X's identity to the police when X, getting wind of this, jammed Miles' head into that gas burner, not knowing that Miles had somehow gotten a letter or document off to Magda, his proof that X had done

117

the murder. Then X had made a date with Magda to meet her at the studio to discuss the letter . . . perhaps, even to buy it from her. When she wouldn't hand it over X had seized the purse which contained whatever it was the murderer wanted and shoved Magda through the window. That was my theory, the police's theory, too. But suppose Miles had killed Ella and then died of a heart attack and that Y, for reasons unknown, killed Magda? Or suppose . . . But I made up my mind not to think of any more difficulties. First, I would follow the obvious line; if that failed . . . well, it *wouldn't* fail. As I look back on it now, I think my confidence in myself at that point was remarkably unjustified.

I had reason to believe from Gleason's behavior that morning at the inquest that he was planning to make an arrest in the next twenty-four hours . . . Elmer Bush had said as much in his column and he had undoubtedly got it from the horse's ass. I looked at my watch. Three-thirty. I had less than a day in which to find the murderer.

I spent about twenty valuable minutes on the telephone, lining up the suspects, making appointments for spurious reasons. Then I told the duo-typists that they would see me no more that day. If the Press wanted news, I recommended they contact Gleason, or Elmer Bush. Miss Flynn wished me luck.

Eglanova's maid let me in without comment. I sometimes wonder if she knows any English. From the bathroom I heard Eglanova's voice above a Niagara of bathwater. 'Peter! I am right out in one minute!'

The maid withdrew and, feeling like a Pinkerton man, I covered the living room and the bedroom with the speed of an Electrolux vacuum cleaner. Needless to say, I found nothing of interest. The rooms were an old-fashioned clutter of photographs and bric-a-brac and antimacassars, establishing, as her legs did not, that Eglanova was an Edwardian, a displaced person in time.

'If I keep you waiting, I am sorry,' she said, sweeping down on me in a creation of mauve satin, her head wrapped in a towel. 'I wash my hair. First, soap and water. Then gasoline. Gives marvelous luster. Even during the war I use gasoline. I tell authorities Eglanova's hair important, too. They give me little coupon book . . . so nice of them. And people say Americans are barbarians!' She sat down in her usual place by the window.

I sat opposite her. The inevitable hot tea and lemon was brought us.

'You like nougat?'

I shook my head and watched, fascinated, while she devoured two large awful-looking pieces of nougat. 'From admirer,' she said, her mouth full. 'He sends me nougat from Rome, Italy. Only place for nougat . . . and Parma violets: I eat pound of violets at one sitting once when I dance in Florence.'

'I'll stick to tea.'

'You never be big and strong,' she said and took a swig of tea. Outside the sun glared, like a globe of brass in the afternoon.

I decided the direct approach was best. 'I think they're going to arrest Jane.'

Eglanova blinked, as though I had made a move to strike her. Unsteadily, she put her tea beside the gaily painted nougat box on a marble-topped table. 'What . . . why you think this?'

'She's being watched every second by a plainclothes man . . . the way they watched Miles when he was to be arrested.'

Eglanova smiled wryly. 'They watch me, too, Peter. I am no fool. I know all along they suspect me. I have engaged two lawyers . . . in case.'

'Yes, they suspect you, too, but they're making a case against Jane. Like a fool, she went to see Miles the evening he was killed, or died. She was with Magda in that classroom before Magda died!'

'But, child, she is so safe! She had no reason to kill Sutton. She never has reason. Surely even that brute who asks questions must know this thing.'

'I'm sure he knows it and I'm also sure that he has to arrest somebody or there'll be trouble for him and the police department, from the papers, from the public.'

'So they give her trial and she is innocent.'

'In the meantime her reputation is ruined. All her life people will say: "Oh, yes, she was mixed up in that ballet murder." Because by the time the case falls flat, the real murderer will have covered his tracks and the case might never be solved and she'll always be suspected. People will say a smart lawyer got her out of it. You know the way they talk. They always want to believe the worst.'

'Poor little Jane.'

'I want to stop it before we really have to say poor little Jane.'

Eglanova laughed. 'And I help you? They arrest poor Anna Eglanova instead?'

'They would never arrest you.'

'I am not so sure of that. Of course I did not kill this vile woman but I tell you one thing: if I did kill her I would do such good job there be no talk of murder. I know ways,' and looking like a real murderess she shut those Asiatic eyes of hers until they were like black slanting lines drawn on her white face.

'Then who did kill her?'

'Meaning if I did not? Ah, you are not gallant.'

'No, I didn't mean that.'

'I don't know. I think sometimes I know but I am afraid . . . very afraid.'

'Think back to the night at the theater. Can't you remember anything which might help us, you and Jane and me?'

'I try. God, how I try all time! I go to Greek church and pray something happen . . . that whole thing be forgotten by a miracle. But no miracle, and I remember nothing. I am in dressing room almost all time. I go for little dinner across the street. I come back. I stay in dressing room. Why I never even know where cable is until afterward. After all, I am not in ballet. I pay no attention to ballets in which I am not dancing. I had no idea I was connected with whole thing until Ivan told me about shears and how you save me embarrassment. For which I am so grateful.'

'Then try and help now.'

'I pray for miracle. Otherwise I can do nothing.' She had never seemed so oriental to me before . . . like a peasant woman in Samarkand.

'Who do you think killed Ella?'

She looked away, very pale. 'Don't ask me this question.'

'But you want to help.'

'Not like this . . . not to hurt people I care about.'

'If you don't help, Jane will be hurt . . . maybe you will be, too.'

'I have good lawyers,' she mumbled, looking away, out the window at the sunlit yard, at the garbage pails gleaming dully in the light.

'And so has Jane,' I lied. 'We've already discussed what their strategy will be if she is indicted. They intend to incriminate *you* as the person with the greatest single motive.' This was wild but it had the effect I wanted.

Her head jerked around toward me and the narrow eyes opened wide . . . I saw, I think for the first time, that Eglanova's eyes were as grey as metal, as silver as steel.

'Let them. I am not afraid.'

'Not even of the publicity, of the months in and out of court? Because they won't be able to convict her and they'll indict you next and maybe they'll be able to make the conviction stick, lawyers or no lawyers.' It is not possible for a white face to turn pale but if it were I could have seen the change right then and there . . . as it was her face sagged.

'Then they find out truth,' she said at last, slowly, looking at me all the time with those silver cat's eyes of hers.

'And the truth?'

'Don't you know? Can't you guess? It is so plain. It is why I have not slept for weeks. Why I grow sick. Why I almost fall off *arabesque* in *Swan Lake* on the last night . . . I am so weak . . . not because those terrible men throw things at stage, like I said, but because I am frightened for some person I adore!'

'For whom?'

'For Alyosha.'

I said nothing for several minutes and Eglanova, as though shocked herself by the enormity of what she had said, drank tea quickly, a thin trickle of it on her chin.

'Why did he do this?' I asked at last, softly, respectful of the panic which had brought her to make such an admission.

'We were married,' she said at last. 'For a number of years. I am bad on time. I don't remember how many years, but a long time, in this country, after I come with Grand Saint Petersburg from Paris. Then we grow apart. He is old man and I am young woman. He is tired and I am in my prime so we part, on good terms. I have my private life but I do not marry again. Alyosha falls in love with Ella and he loves her a long time, but like an old man . . . a mistake I tell him but he doesn't listen, no, he thinks he can hold this little *corps de ballet* girl, but of course, she sees better opportunity and marries Miles, poor stupid Miles, who is fooled by tricks as old as woman. Then she becomes great star and Alyosha hates her, worse even than Miles. And he comes to me and I comfort him . . . we have no bitterness. Alyosha and I. He is like a brother to me always. When Washburn tries to replace me with Sutton, Alyosha is just like a madman . . .'

'And Alyosha killed Ella?'

She nodded, not looking at me. 'I think that is what happened.'

'Do you mean to tell me that after he killed Ella he put the murder weapon in your room . . . to throw suspicion on you?'

'I don't know . . . I don't know . . . I don't know what happened after that . . . maybe he uses something else to cut with. I only tell you all this now because I have very little time, because I can dance only one two more seasons and because I have so little time I cannot be involved for many months in courts, with lawyers. I put dance ahead of Alyosha . . . ahead of me, child, ahead of everything. It is the big thing . . . and though I love Alyosha I never ask him to kill this Sutton.' She stopped abruptly and put her empty tea glass on the table with a click. 'He was not wise but he is old man and very bitter. You should have seen him the way he was in Russia . . . yes, I am almost old myself. I remember him when he was young dancer . . . so handsome, such man! you have never seen such man! Women, men, children they fall in love with him, follow him in streets everywhere he goes. Then we leave Russia and go on tour and all Europe loves him. Not because he is such good dancer like Nijinski but because he is so beautiful, because he is so good . . . but that was a long time ago, child. We are old now.' And I saw the tears in her eyes. She did not speak to me again and so, with a murmured good-by, I left her.

2

I had made a date to see Jed Wilbur after rehearsal, at four-thirty. I arrived at the studio just as the place was breaking up. It looked strange seeing our dancers in their tights running in and out between plainclothes men in double-breasted suits with snap-brim hats worn like uniform caps.

I said hello to Jane who was standing by the drinking fountain reading the rehearsal schedule with a preoccupied frown.

'How did it go?' I asked.

She jumped. 'Oh, it's you. I'm like a cat today. It went O.K. Nobody was thinking about the ballet except Wilbur.'

'What's the ballet like?'

'I don't remember a thing.' She shuddered. 'That policeman! He gives me the shivers. For some reason he's decided that I know a great deal more about all this than I do. He's been asking me questions all morning. Where was I at such a time, how well I know Ella . . . as if I had anything to do with this mess. I couldn't get it through his head that my only connection with the murder was through Magda who was a friend of mine and not much of a friend . . . I mean she latched on to me during her troubles with Miles just because I'm so goddamned sympathetic.'

'I don't suppose it's any use my telling you again what a mistake you made in going to Miles' apartment that night, and not telling Gleason about it . . .'

'No use at all. What are you doing right now?'

'I have to see Wilbur on business. Then I'm off to dinner with some people . . . newspaper people. I don't know when I'll be back.'

'Try and finish early. I'm going to be home all evening. I don't know when I've ever been so jittery.'

I said that I would and she disappeared into the ladies' dressing room. I was about to go into the studio where I could see Wilbur talking to some dancers, when Louis hove-to, flashing that ivory smile . . . uncapped teeth, by the way.

'What's new, Baby?'

'About that Harlem deal,' I said. 'I'd like to go up there some time.'

'That's a good boy. I knew you come around.' He gave me a sweaty hug. 'We go tonight . . . unless you rather go straight on to my place.'

'I'd like to see Harlem first. I'm writing a book.'

'That's a hot one,' said Louis who liked only comic books about Superman and Prince Valiant and Terry and the Pirates. We made a date to meet at eleven in the Algonquin lobby.

I avoided Gleason who was, I gathered, in the classroom sifting evidence. Wilbur had obviously forgotten our appointment but he was pleasant enough and suggested I go to his apartment with him while he changed clothes.

Jed lived in a small apartment in one of the drearier housing projects on the East Side . . . one of those red brick fortress jobs with tiny windows, the perfect place for a true liberal to get that anthill feeling, that sense of oneness with everyman.

I sat in his living room while he showered and dressed. I cased everything, much the way I had in Eglanova's apartment, and with the same result. It is difficult to search a room for nothing in particular; on the other hand, you get some feeling of the owner's character. In this case, a rather negative feeling. Everything was functional, 1930-modern, lots of chrome and natural-wood finishes and no decorations other than an abstract painting on the wall, so abstract that it would take an art-lover more dedicated than I to tell whether it was good or bad. In the bookcase were twenty or thirty books on ballet, and nothing else. I was quite sure that the inevitable reference works of the left wing could be found in the bedroom, hidden away while the heat was on.

'I've never been so tired,' said Wilbur, coming back into the room wearing a T-shirt and a pair of slacks which hung loosely from his thin body. 'Want a drink?' We had bourbon and water.

Then he sat at the other end of the grey and gold couch and looked at me expectantly.

'It's about these Washington hearings,' I said. 'I wanted to know when you were going down and when you'd be back and how you'd like us to handle the publicity . . . especially for Chicago where we may run into trouble. You see, Mr. Washburn has dropped the whole public relations end in my lap and I don't quite know how to handle it.' I was dazzlingly glib.

'I wish I knew what to say,' said Wilbur, twisting a lock of hair. 'Because of this murder business I can't go away yet. It takes precedence, I gather, over a Congressional subpoena. I suppose, though, that as soon as they arrest whoever they're planning to, I'll be able to go down, testify, and be back in a couple of days. Don't worry; they won't find anything. Try and

124

convince that fool Washburn, if you can. I'm sure he thinks I'm a Russian spy.'

'He's an alarmist.'

'This mess all dates back to my connection with the North American Ballet. Two of the dancers were party members and the rest of us were sympathizers . . . I've already admitted that a hundred times. Unfortunately this is a competitive business and people have been trying to knock me off for years. If you get to the top they'll use any stick to beat you with. This Communist scare was made to order for my enemies. But I'll lick them yet; if I have to go through a thousand investigations.' Wilbur was properly truculent and I couldn't help but admire his spirit. He was not going to knuckle under; the toughness that had got him where he was hadn't deserted him. I felt, though, that he tended to over-dramatize the situation . . . I mean, after all, who really gives a damn about a choreographer, a dancing master, a twinkle-toes expert; it's a minor art form in a second-rate theater, for which sentiment I could probably be run out of town.

'Have you much to do with Gleason?' I asked, before he could go into the inevitable. 'I-am-a-suffering-artist-who-has-struggled-to-bring-beauty-into-the-world' routine that so many of our talented corn balls slip into at a moment's notice.

'Gleason?' He looked bewildered, the autobiography of Jed Wilbur mid-twentieth-century choreographer, halted at the first chapter. 'You mean that Inspector? No, not since yesterday when he had us all in. I've got enough to worry about without getting mixed up in these murders. Do you realize that they may not let us go to Chicago next week? That my ballet may not be ready even if we do go, what with all these damned interruptions? It was godawful today . . . I can tell you that. The company was worse than usual . . . if that could be possible. It was like running through molasses. I'll tell you one thing, though, which I haven't even told brother Washburn; if we're not allowed to go to Chicago I'm going to break my contract. I've already talked to my lawyer and he says that I've a legal right to.'

'I'm sure Gleason will have solved the case by then, before the Chicago opening.'

'I hope so.' Wilbur poured himself another drink.

'Who do you think did it?' My question was abrupt.

'Did what? The murders? I haven't the slightest idea. Tell me

125

did that ape from the Veterans' Committee show up today . . . what's his name, Fleer?'

'I don't think so. Mr. Washburn and I sent away most of the callers . . . including the Press.'

'He has a personal grudge against me. I swear he has. This is downright persecution. Why, of all the liberals in New York, in the theater, did he have to go after me? The one who really cares just about as much about politics as . . . as Eglanova.'

'After all you said yourself the reason . . . I mean, you're the first in your profession. You're a big target. If they could knock you off that would really be something for them . . . a real victory. Justify their whole existence.'

This neatly tendered wreath of laurel was received in grateful silence as he absorbed my statement about his pre-eminent position in the ballet: Wilbur . . . then Tudor, Balanchine, Ashton, Robbins. This brief meditation put him in a good humor. His expression grew more gentle, almost relaxed.

I repeated my earlier question.

'Who killed Ella and the others? Well, I'm not sure that any opinion I would have would be worth a damn. You see, I'm new to the company. I don't have much idea of all the politics and so forth. . . . As a matter of fact, I've been so involved in my own mess that I haven't paid as much attention to all this as I probably should. But just remember that it isn't easy to create two ballets, defend your reputation and worry about a few murders, too. I figure if I survive the next month I'm going to Bermuda for the rest of the summer, right after the Chicago première. I can't take much more.'

'But you have known all the people involved for a long time. The ballet's a pretty small world no matter which company you're with.'

'That's true. But ballet companies are like families. They are different on the inside . . . no matter how well you know them from the outside.'

'You knew Ella a long time?'

'Oh yes. In fact, except for Louis, she was the person I knew best in the company.'

'How long did you know her?'

'You sound just like that policeman.' He smiled at me.

'I'm pretty concerned. This is my bread and butter. You can

126

always go on to another company, to Broadway. I'm on a salary, and there aren't many jobs around as pleasant as this.'

'I see what you mean. O.K. . . . Ella Sutton. How long did I know her? Since Nineteen Thirty-Seven, when she was in the North American Ballet. She joined it the month it folded; even so she danced several leads and got her first recognition.'

'Did you see much of her after that?'

'Very little. We never worked together from that day until she got Washburn to hire me to make some new ballets for her.'

'I didn't know Ella was responsible for hiring you.'

'She was indeed. I suspect she was the most ambitious dancer in the history of ballet. She felt she had mastered the classics and the Grand Saint Petersburg chestnuts; she wanted to branch out . . . to prove she was a great dramatic dancer like Nora Kaye. So she got Washburn to hire me . . . for which I could kill her. . . .' He laughed, suddenly aware of what he had said. 'If somebody hadn't taken care of that already. As far as I'm concerned, in spite of the success of *Eclipse*, my little association with your company has taken ten years off my life.'

'Did you like Ella?'

'Certainly not. She was a bitch, not at all the kind of woman I like,' he said, making a perfunctory effort to show his aversion to Ella was not a general one, did not include the entire sex . . . which of course it did. 'But she was one marvelous dancer. I felt, working with her this season, that she might easily have become the finest ballerina of our time . . . and I've worked with the whole lot, with just about every important dancer in the world.'

'Who do you think killed her?'

He frowned; then he finished his drink. 'You know,' he said at last, 'I've gotten so nervous lately with all these investigations that I hardly dare open my mouth to say it's a warm day for fear some bastard will twist what I say around and use it against me.'

'Well, there're only two of us here. You need two witnesses, don't you, to prove a statement? You can tell me what you think, if you want to.'

'Then I may as well say what I think . . . not what I *know*; and if you quote me on this I'll deny it till I'm blue in the face. From what little I know of this company and the way it's put together, I'd say the Russians did it.'

'Eglanova?'

'And Alyosha . . . one or the other or both. I mean who else had any real motive? Aside from Miles, and I still think maybe *he* did it; though that makes Magda's death seem a little crazy . . . which makes me also think that the whole thing might be the work of a lunatic. God knows we have enough of them in ballet —and more than our share in this company.'

'I don't think Eglanova would ever take such a chance.'

'It wasn't much of a chance since she knew Miles would be blamed for it, as he was. Or maybe she had Alyosha do it for her. He certainly hated Ella . . . though I suppose if he did it he wouldn't have planted those shears in Eglanova's room. That's more the sort of thing *she* might've done, an obvious stunt to make herself seem victimized. But that's all theorizing. Ideally, I'd be very happy if the police just gave up, or arrested the janitor, somebody who didn't have a thing to do with ballet but if they have to arrest the old girl, or Alyosha, I wish they'd hurry up and do it so I can go to Washington and clear myself. I don't want anything to affect my chances for the fall, with that musical . . . it's the biggest chance I've had in the commercial theater and I'm looking forward to it . . . and not just to the money either. . . . It's a chance to do something big . . . something nobody else has done before.'

He talked awhile about the great things he intended to do; I then asked him if the rumor I'd heard about Louis' going into musical comedy was true.

'Where did you hear that?'

'Some of the boys in the company . . . you know how they chatter.'

'We talked about it once. I don't think he wants to leave the ballet.'

'He'd be good in musicals,' I said.

'You never can tell.' Then Wilbur steered the subject back to himself and before I left he had given me a number of pronouncements to give to the Press about his political status.

3

It was almost seven o'clock when I met Alyosha at the Russian Tea Room on Fifty-seventh Street, a favourite meeting place for the ballet, where the Russians often sit for hours at a time drinking tea and eating pressed caviar.

I found Alyosha at his usual table, just inside the main room. He was going through his mail when I joined him; he was as dapper as ever, his monocle in place, a glass of vodka at his elbow. I remember thinking at the time that if he was a murderer, he was certainly a cool one. Except for the marks of fatigue which were standard equipment for the members of the Grand Saint Petersburg Ballet Company that season, he could not have been more relaxed as he motioned me to the chair opposite him.

'I'm sorry I'm late,' I said, ordering bourbon. 'But I've been at the office, trying to keep the newspapers in line.'

'They are like wolves,' said the old gentleman, placing a cigarette in his long onyx holder. 'They smell blood and they want more of it.'

'I know one thing: they're crazy for an arrest.'

'And this Inspector plans to give them one, I am sure.'

'The wrong one, too, I'll bet.'

'Undoubtedly,' said Alyosha sadly.

'I wish I could head them off.'

'How?'

'I don't know. I only meant I *wished* I could . . . because of Jane.'

'Is she involved?'

I was quick enough, fortunately, to get out of that one. I did some extraordinary feints and maneuvers. 'We're going to be married,' I said. 'And all this is making things so difficult for us . . . her being in Wilbur's new ballet . . . the strain of doing *Eclipse* night after night, terrified that someone may do the same thing to her that they did to Sutton. Well, it isn't the most wonderful climate for love.'

'Love makes its own climate,' said Alyosha with a warm smile. 'Let me congratulate you.'

'Thank you . . . I appreciate that. . . . But don't say anything to the company about it . . . for now.'

'I shall be very discreet.' He toasted me in tea and I toasted him in bourbon. We talked for a while of love and marriage and he told me about himself and Eglanova. 'What a divine woman she is! I have never known any woman so without vanity or meanness. Oh, I know that seems strange since she is such an egotist about her work, but that is natural. . . . It is the ballet she cares about, not Eglanova. In a way it is like the priesthood for her, for us. You Americans are not quite the same thing. You think of money and glamour and all that, not of the thing itself, the dance, the work, the magic. In a way our marriage was perfect.'

'But it ended.'

'All things must . . . in our world sooner than later. I was infatuated with someone else and so it ended. Yet Anna never reproached me, not once.'

'With Ella?'

'Yes . . . I am afraid everyone knows. I made a fool of myself, but I don't blame *her*. We were such different people. I thought first of ballet then of her and she thought only of herself; she thought because I loved her I'd give her the great roles but I saw that she wasn't ready and I refused, thinking that ballet came first with her, too, that she would know, as I knew, that she wasn't ready. So she married Miles and suddenly, pouf! like that, she *was* ready; overnight she was a great ballerina. Sad woman . . . she ended the way she deserved.'

'Did you hate her so?'

'For a long time but not in the last year. I felt something would happen . . . I am not superstitious but I think sometimes a terrible deed casts a shadow before it. I saw the shadow some time ago. I knew she would not be allowed to live much longer . . . and I was sorry for her. After all, I had loved her once.'

'I have some news,' I said, interrupting this mystical reverie.

'News?' He put the onyx holder down and looked at me politely.

'The police are going to arrest the murderer tomorrow.'

'How do you know?'

'I found out this afternoon . . . through the grapevine . . . the warrant is being prepared now.'

'But they *can't* do this to her . . . they can't!' He fell with the grace of a dying swan into my little trap . . . unless of course I had fallen into *his* trap; at the moment, I wasn't sure which, but I bluffed it through.

'I'm afraid they can. After all, even a great dancer like Eglanova is at the mercy of the law.'

'I know, but we must stop them.' He let his monocle drop; he was suddenly haggard-looking. 'She mustn't be brought to trial.'

'But if she's innocent she'll be let off.'

'Innocent!' he groaned.

'Do you think she really killed Ella?'

'Who else?' His voice was strained and it quavered; he sounded very old.

'Did you talk to her about it?'

'Never. We have never discussed Ella alone together since it happened. I knew. She knew that I knew, from the beginning. There was never anything to say.'

'Did you talk like this to Gleason?'

'Of course not. I made up lies! oh, such lies, such confusion! They may never straighten out all the things I tell them.'

'Even so they will arrest her tomorrow.'

'Then we must get Ivan. We must engage lawyers. The best in America . . . I am told in this country with a good lawyer you can escape anything.'

'It's been known to happen. She already knows the police suspect her, but they may arrest her any minute.'

'I should be with her now.'

'I'm not sure that'd be such a good idea.' For the moment, I didn't want any of these people getting together and comparing notes; if they did I might find myself in serious trouble. 'You see the police are watching her and if they think you might be an accomplice of some sort your testimony in her favor won't be worth a cent.'

'Even so . . .'

'Besides, she told me she was going to be with her lawyers this evening. Wait until tomorrow. That's the only thing to do, the only really intelligent thing to do . . .' I talked for several minutes, trying to divert him; then, still unsure as to whether I had or not, I left.

4

Mr. Washburn arrived ten minutes late for dinner with me at a little French restaurant on Fifty-fifth Street. A place with good food and dim lights.

'Elmer Bush is going to drop by in an hour,' said Mr. Washburn, sitting down, not even bothering to say good evening.

'Is that a good idea?'

'Good idea or not we have to see him. He's in charge around here, just as much as Gleason.' This last name, on his lips, became a curse.

We ordered a light cool dinner. The room was dark but not air-conditioned . . . it was a little like being in a cave somewhere in Africa.

'The police are going to make an arrest, aren't they?'

He nodded.

'Jane?'

'I'm doing everything I can to stop it. I've been at City Hall all afternoon. I've talked to the Mayor, to the Governor up in Albany.'

'I suggest you find her a good lawyer.'

'Benson will represent her . . . I've seen to that, at company expense.' I knew then he was serious; Mr. Washburn doesn't like to spend money.

'Jane doesn't know yet, does she?'

'I don't think so. *You're* the one who sees her.'

'She's home now. She suspects they might . . . it's so damned awful, so stupid! Didn't you explain to Gleason that there is no motive, absolutely none? That regardless of circumstantial evidence, the state is going to look damned funny when they try to convict her?'

'He seems confident.'

'But can't you stop him? A trial like this could ruin her.'

'I can't do anything more than get her acquitted. She *will* be acquitted . . . I'm sure of that.'

It's a good thing, I suppose, that I have a great deal of self-control because my impulse at that moment was to rush straight to Gleason's office and tell him exactly what I thought of his investigation.

'Besides,' said Mr. Washburn, 'I have reason to believe that the trial will be speeded up so that Jane will be through in time for our Los Angeles opening.'

I was beginning, dimly, to see the plot. 'You seem very confident,' I said, 'that by the time the trial is over the police will have lost interest in the case . . . that Eglanova will be out of danger.' I was now fully aware that Jane was to be the lightning rod for the whole company in general and for Eglanova in particular.

'I don't know what you're talking about,' said my employer sharply and I shut up. There was plenty of time for saying what I had to say.

We ate the first course in silence; then, when the entree arrived, I asked, very casually, 'Tell me, Mr. Washburn, why you were trying to get Armiger to take Eglanova's place, before Ella was killed.'

I suppose if I had spat in his face I would have made less effect; he sat back in his chair abruptly and his chin jerked up, like a boxer off guard.

'How did you know I'd written her?'

'I saw her answer on your desk one day.'

'I'm not sure I approve of your reading my mail.'

'It was accidental, believe me. I don't usually read other people's mail. I've been wondering, though . . . been wondering quite a bit lately whether that might tie in with the murders. You see, it's more important to me to get Jane off the hook than it is for you to save Eglanova.'

'You haven't mentioned seeing that letter to anyone, have you?'

'Not yet. But I plan to tell Gleason about it tomorrow . . . any stunt I can think of to throw him off the track.'

'It could be misinterpreted.' Mr. Washburn was worried.

'It would provide a mild diversion. They might even suspect you.'

Washburn snorted. 'As if I would make such trouble for myself! All I have to do is *fire* a ballerina . . . it couldn't be simpler. I don't have to kill them . . . though there are times when I have been greatly tempted.'

'Why did you write Armiger?'

'Because right after we opened in New York, Sutton told me that she and Louis were planning to quit the company and go into musical comedy, into night clubs, to make money. I was furious of course; I did all I could to stop her, promised her more money than Eglanova gets . . . everything, but she said she'd made up her mind.'

'Then that clears you.'

'Not entirely,' said Mr. Washburn very distinctly, his eyes on mine. 'I found out after I wrote to Armiger that Ella had said

133

nothing to Louis about this plan of hers . . . or rather they had discussed it but neither, according to him, had decided to leave the company. For some reason she wanted to upset me, to get me to promise her more money which I did and which I was bound to give her after Eglanova left. That's the way the situation was when she died. She hadn't told me she would stay with us but I knew, after talking to Louis, that she would. . . .'

'But in the meantime you had written that letter to Armiger.'

'To several other dancers, too.'

'Very messy.'

'I sometimes wish I had stayed in Bozeman.'

'Stayed where?'

'Bozeman, Montana. That's where I was born. . . . I still own property there. I came East about twenty years ago and my ex-wife got me into ballet.' This was an unexpected confidence. As a rule, Mr. Washburn never made any references to his life before the ballet, nor could one find out much about him before his ballet days. I know. I tried soon after I joined the company; out of curiosity, I looked him up and found almost nothing at all. His birthplace is recorded, officially, as San Francisco, the child of Anglo-Russian parents; his mother was supposed to have been a dancer called the 'Pearl of the Baltic'. None of this of course was true . . . a real New York biography! much glamour and no facts.

'In a way,' said Mr. Washburn after a brief reminiscence or two on his early days, 'this may be a blessing for all of us.'

'What may be?'

'Their putting Jane on trial. They haven't a chance in the world of making any case against her stick because she is so obviously innocent and, let's face it, of almost all the people involved in this business she is the one least likely to be hurt by a trial. They might make a case against Eglanova or Alyosha or even against me, and make it stick regardless of how innocent we are in fact . . .'

'But is Eglanova innocent?'

'I have never allowed myself to think of her or anyone else connected with my company as a murderer.'

'Then you should allow yourself to think right now that somebody we both know *is* responsible for those murders and that Jane is scheduled to take the rap for that somebody. It might be a good policy for us to co-operate with Gleason and help

134

him catch the real murderer instead of trying to confuse him the way you've been doing for the last few weeks, helping him make a case against Jane whom you know is innocent.'

'I've done no such thing. I . . .'

'Then why did you tell Gleason about seeing Jane at Miles' apartment? Especially when you made it a point to tell me you *hadn't* mentioned it to Gleason.' This was wild but I had to take chances; it worked.

'I didn't want to upset you and then have you disturb Jane when she was working on a new ballet. Of course I told Gleason. How would it have looked if I hadn't? He knew anyway.'

'I don't like this . . .'

'In which case you may want to find a job somewhere else,' said Mr. Washburn looking at me coldly, a piece of lettuce sticking to his lower lip.

'I have other jobs,' I said brazenly. 'Which is fortunate . . . especially if they start investigating those letters you wrote Armiger and the other dancers.'

'Are you trying to blackmail me? Because if you are . . .'

'Christ no!' I said. 'I'm just trying to make a little sense out of the mess you and the others have made. I don't know why but it seems that everybody connected with this company has a constitutional aversion to telling the truth which is very nearly miraculous . . . I mean just by accident the truth will sometimes out, but not in this set. I'm sick to death of all the shenanigans . . . yours, too, Mr. Washburn.'

'A fine speech,' said Elmer Bush appearing out of the shadows.

'A little joke,' said Mr. Washburn easily, getting to his feet. 'How are you, Elmer? Let me order you a drink.'

'The boy may be right,' said Elmer, accepting a gin and tonic from a waiter. 'Sometimes it's best to be direct.'

'He's very much upset, as he should be.'

'Over that girl? Well, he has every reason to be,' said Elmer Bush, giving me his serious television gaze, the one denoting sympathy, compassion.

'What do you mean?' I asked, knowing exactly what he meant.

'You better get her a good lawyer; she'll need one, starting tomorrow.'

'I've got Benson for her,' said Mr. Washburn. 'And of course we'll take care of the bond.'

'She's innocent,' I said wearily.

'Perhaps,' said Elmer Bush, 'but the police and the Press both think she killed Ella to get her part in that ballet.'

'Thin motive, isn't it?'

'They may have evidence we know nothing about,' said Elmer, looking as though he knew all sorts of things nobody else did . . . which was possible. If it was, I had another puzzle dropped in my lap . . . and there wasn't much time to unravel all the threads, to work everything out.

'Do you mind,' said Mr. Washburn, turning to me with icy formality. 'Elmer and I . . .'

'I'm on my way,' I said, getting to my feet. I gave them a brisk good night. Then I headed down the street to the Blue Angel. There, sitting in a booth at a black table under a red light, I pulled out my sheet of paper and began to go over the names, solving some of the old mysteries, adding the new ones I'd come across during the evening, making brief notes on my conversations with the suspects. While make those notes, I figured out who killed Ella Sutton. There was the solution in front of me, in black and white. The only bad thing was that I didn't have one bit of evidence to prove what I knew. I was very pleased with myself; I was also scared to death.

VII

I DOUBT whether I will ever forget that evening I spent with Louis; we did New York from the Village to Harlem in something under nine hours, from eleven-thirty that night to eight-thirty the next morning when I crawled off to bed.

We met at the Algonquin. From there we went to a bar in the Village . . . Hermione's I think it's called.

I thought I knew a great deal about our feathered friends, the shy, sensitive dancers and so on that I've met these last few years in New York, but that night with Louis was an eye-opener . . . it was like those last chapters in Proust when everybody around starts turning into boy-lovers until there isn't a womanizer left on deck.

'You'll like this bar,' said Louis with a happy grin as he marched me into a long blue-lit tunnel, an upholstered sewer, with a number of tables in back and a bar in front. Heads turned to look at us; there was a hiss of recognition when they saw Louis. He's hot stuff in these circles.

We pushed our way to the back of the bar and a mincing youth, a waiter, found us a table right by the stage, a wooden platform about four feet square with a microphone in front of it and a piano beside it. The stage was empty. A tired little man sat at the piano, banging away.

'They have a swell show here,' said my guide.

'What will it be, big boy?' said Mae West, behind me; I turned and saw that it wasn't Miss West . . . only our waiter who despite his debutante slouch managed to give a vivid impersonation of that great American Lady.

Louis ordered gin and I ordered a coke, to Louis' horror but I was firm . . . I had no intention of getting tanked tonight, for a number of reasons, all good.

The pianist, getting a look at Louis, played a hopped-up version of *Swan Lake* in his honor and a more godawful noise I've never heard. He was rewarded with a big smile from the French Nijinski.

'Nice, isn't it? They know me here even though I only get down this way maybe once twice a season.'

'Tell me, Louis, how does it feel to be famous?' And believe it or not he told me; it was the last time I ever tried irony on that boy . . . on any dancer because, for some reason or another, they are the most literal-minded crew in the world.

When he had finished telling me what it was like at the end of a ballet when the applause was coming up out of the darkened house ('like waves'), our waiter eased by with the drinks as I watched, fascinated. Most queens walk in a rather trotting manner with necks and shoulders rigid, like women, and the lower anatomy swiveling a bit; not our waiter, though . . . he was like Theda Bara moving in for a couple of million at the box office, in the days when a dollar was a dollar.

'Here's your poison,' he said in that slow Mae Western manner of his.

'That's a boy,' said Louis and he swallowed a shot of gin which he immediately chased with a mouthful of water. He grimaced. 'Lighter fluid,' he said.

'What did you expect, lover, ambrosia?' Obviously a literary belle, our waiter . . . and what a joy it was to hear her say 'ambrosia'!

'Just a little old-fashioned gin.'

'You want some more?'

'The real stuff.'

The belle looked at him beneath sleepy lids which even in the dim light I could see had been heavily mascaraed. 'Are you *that dancer*?'

'That's me.' And Louis flashed the ivory smile.

'That's what Mary said when you came in but I said, no, this one's too old.'

One for the belle, I said to myself, as Louis' smile vanished. 'Get the gin,' he said, suddenly rough and surly.

'I didn't mean any offense,' said the belle, with a smile of triumph; she ambled off swaying like some tall flower in a summer breeze.

'Bitch,' said Louis, in a bad temper. But then two admirers came over, college boy types, very young and drunk.

'Hey, you Louis Giraud aren't you?' asked one of them, a crewcut number, short and stocky. The other was a gentle-looking blond.

138

'Yes,' said Louis, obviously taking no chances after his experience with the waiter.

'See, what did I say?' said the short one to the tall one.

'He's kidding you,' said the blond.

'No, he's not,' I said, just to be helpful; Louis was beginning to look very tough indeed.

'Giraud's right calf is about half an inch thicker than his left,' said the blond.

I could tell by the gleam in his eye that he was a balleto-mane.

'Please show us,' said the short one. 'I got a bet . . .'

Louis, exhibitionist to the last, pulled up his trouser legs to reveal those massive legs, like blue marble in this light; sure enough one calf was bigger than the other. They both touched him very carefully, like children in a museum. 'I win,' said the short one and he pulled the taller one away, with some difficulty now that Louis' identity had been established.

'Nice boys,' said Louis, with his old good humor. 'Like little pussycats, fuzzy and nice.'

'They don't look much like pussycats to me,' I said austerely.

'Why don't you come off it, Baby? Stop all this girl-business.'

'I can't help it, Louis. I got a weak character.'

'I could teach you a lot,' said Louis with a speculative look; before he could start the first lesson, however, the belle returned with another shot of gin.

'Compliments of the management, Miss Pavlova,' said the belle insolently.

'Why don't you go stuff . . .'

'That's no way to talk to a lady,' said the belle, with a far-away Blanche Dubois smile.

But then the chief entertainer Molly Malloy came over, a man in his late thirties with small regular features; he was wearing a crimson evening gown and a blond wig like Jean Harlow.

'Hi, there, Louis, long time no see,' said Molly in a husky voice, not precisely female but on the other hand not very male either. He sat down at our table, drawing all eyes toward us. I felt very self-conscious.

'How're you doing, Molly? I've been all tied up all season . . . haven't been able to get out once.'

'That's not what I hear. This your new chick?' asked Molly, giving me the eye.

'Yeah,' said Louis, beaming. 'Pretty cute piece, huh?'

'Well you always get the best, dear. And I know why.' There was much vulgar laughter and I looked politely away, looked toward the bar where youths and old men of every description were furtively nudging one another, all engaged in the maneuvers of courtship. It was a very interesting thing to watch.

'You still doing the same act, Molly?'

'Haven't changed it in ten years . . . my public wouldn't let me . . . even if I could. Tell me, dear, about all that excitement you've been having uptown: all those dancers murdering each other. Who did it?'

'Damned if I know,' said Louis, and he changed the subject, the way he had with me all night whenever I tried to get the conversation around to the murders, tried to question Louis about one or two things which had to be cleared up before I could get the proof I needed. But Louis wasn't talking. And I wasn't giving up . . . not if I had to get him drunk, a hard job but, under the circumstances, a necessary one since I'd heard he talks a lot when he's drunk and there's truth in the grape, as the ancients used to say.

'Well, dear, it's been a real sensation . . . let me tell you. And such publicity! If it doesn't sell tickets my name isn't Molly Malloy.' I couldn't help but wonder whether or not his name really was Molly Malloy. 'Come here, Miss Priss,' said Molly sternly to our waiter who obeyed with the air of a royal princess dispensing favors, or maybe Saint Theresa scrubbing floors. 'Another gin for Louis Giraud the dancer, another coke and a Tom Collins . . . understand?'

'You don't have to act like I was deaf,' said the aggrieved, petulantly; another round was brought us and when Louis finished his third shot of gin he was definitely in a joyous mood . . . just next door to drunkenness and indiscretion. I bided my time.

Then Molly Malloy went into his act, to the delight of the initiates though it was pretty bewildering to me, full of references to people I never heard of, and imitations of celebrated actresses which weren't remotely like the originals, or anything else for that matter. He finished the act with a torch song and, when that was over, disappeared through a door behind the stage to much applause. Beneath clouds of blue smoke the pianist continued to play; voices sounded louder and the mating at the bar grew more intense and indecorous.

During Molly's last number, Louis had taken my hand in his and held it like a vise. After a while I stopped trying to pull away; it wouldn't last forever I knew. That's what I always tell myself in difficult situations, like the war . . . fortunately he soon got tired of kneading my palm and let it drop. I sat on my hands for the next half hour.

'Swell place,' said Louis, after Molly left the stage.

'Swell,' I said.

'I came here on my first night in New York . . . maybe ten years ago. I was just a kid from Europe . . . didn't know a word of English. But I got by.' He laughed. 'Right away a nice old gentleman took me home and since any French boy can make better love than any American, I got me a home real quick; then, later, I go into ballet here . . . to keep busy. I like work . . . work, sleep and . . .' He named his three passions.

'When did you meet Mr. Washburn?' I asked casually.

'When he came backstage at the old ballet company where I was working. I had done one beautiful *Bluebird*; I guess maybe the best damned *Bluebird* since Nijinski. Every company in America was after me. Washburn had the most money so I joined him and he made me *premier danseur*. I like him fine. He treats me like a king.'

'Don't you ever get tired of those old ballets?'

'I hate all new dancing,' said Louis, diverted momentarily from his usual preoccupation with pussycats and such like.

'Even Jed Wilbur's?'

Louis shrugged. 'He's the best of that kind, I guess. I don't get much kick out of dancing in them, though . . . in *Eclipse* and now the new one.'

'Where the father kills the girl, isn't it?'

'I think that's the story. To tell you the truth I don't pay much attention. I just do what they tell me. At least he lets me do things I like to do . . . *tours en l'air*, that kind of thing. He keeps me happy.'

'I wonder what the story means?'

'Why don't you ask Jed? He'll talk your ear off about it. I just go to sleep when he starts getting arty with me.'

'You sound like Eglanova.'

141

He snorted. 'We got that in common then. I love her. She's like a mother to me, ever since I've known her: Louis, you do this, Louis, you do that . . . Louis, don't go out with sailors, Louis, don't snap your head when you finish pirouette, Louis, don't take such deep bows after ballet . . . I never had any mother,' said Louis, and for a minute I thought he was going to have a good cry.

'It's terrible,' I said, 'the way Mr. Washburn tried to get rid of her before Sutton was killed.'

'He's a bastard,' said Louis, gloomily licking the edge of his gin glass. 'He can't help it. He was just made that way . . . all the time doing somebody dirty . . . not that he isn't good to me, as long as I'm hot with the audience. The second I have a little trouble, get bad reviews or something awful, good-by Louis, I know him.'

'He's a businessman.'

'Ballet is art not business,' said Louis making, as far as I knew, his first and last pronouncement on ballet. 'But you should've seen his face when he came to find out if me and Ella were going to quit the company for sure and go into night clubs. He looked like somebody had just belted him one. "Now, Louis, you know we're old friends . . ." that was his line to me; so I strung him along awhile then I told him that Ella was just bluffing him.'

'Do you think she was?'

'At least as far as I was concerned. I didn't have any intention of leaving the company, even though I've thought about it a lot. We had talked a little about it then and just lately Jed has been trying to talk me into doing that big musical of his this fall, but I said no; I mean the money's very nice except that the government gets it all . . . then you're out of a job maybe six months of a year with no money coming in and it isn't so swell. No, I like to know I got a regular amount coming in every week, ten months a year.' I hadn't realized before that Louis was quite so money-conscious, so shrewd.

'I wonder why Ella told Washburn that, about your quitting the company together?'

'Just to worry him a little, to raise her price. She knew he couldn't find another dancer to take her place. As a matter of fact, just between you and me, I think she was planning to leave ballet in a year or so, but alone. I think she wanted to go in musicals and I got a feeling that was why she was so keen on getting Jed to join the company. Oh, she wanted to do a real modern ballet and all that but she wanted to work on him to get her a Broadway job. She had an eye for all the angles.'

'I thought Jed joined the company because of you.'

'You're pretty fresh, *petit gosse*,' said Louis with a grin, pinching my thigh until I just about yelled with pain. 'I wasn't talking about why Jed joined us; I was talking about why Ella wanted him to, why she sold Washburn on the idea.' I rubbed my leg until the pain went away. One day I am going to beat the hell out of Louis, if I can; if I can't I'll do a lot of damage first.

'Jed's sure got it bad for you,' I said in an earnest, slightly breathless tone of voice.

'Funny, isn't it?' said Louis, with a sigh, stretching his arms and controlling a yawn . . . it was stifling in the bar, a single fan made a racket but did not cool the warm smoke-filled air. 'He's been after me for years. Used to write me crazy letters even before we started working together.'

I waved to the waiter who, without asking, brought us another round; before he left he gave Louis a lightning grope and Louis didn't like it but, as I pointed out, he was just getting some of his own medicine. He didn't think that was very funny but after he'd swallowed some more gin he was in a better mood. I tried to get him to talk about Mr. Washburn but he wanted to talk about Jed. 'I'm a lone wolf,' he said, wiping his sweaty face with the back of his hand. 'Lots of guys get themselves a nice pussycat and settle down but not me . . . I used to be a pussycat for some older guys, when I was real young, but I didn't like it much and besides it isn't dignified for a man like me to be kept by somebody else, and that's what Jed's got in mind. He wants me to settle down with him and be his boy while he makes dozens of ballets for me until I'm too old to get around a stage. Even if I liked the idea of going to bed with him, which I don't and never have, I couldn't go for that kind of life and, as for his making ballets for me, well, that's what he's doing right now with Mr. Washburn paying for them in cash, not me paying for them in tail . . . I tell him all this a thousand times but he doesn't listen. He's made up his mind I'm his big love and there's nothing I can do about it. You'd think somebody who'd been around dancers as long as he has wouldn't feel that way, like a little girl, but he's got a one-track mind. He came to us just because I was in the company . . . not because Ella wanted him or because Washburn offered him a lot of money. Believe me it's been hell dodging him, too. I can't take my clothes off but what he isn't in the dressing room wrestling around. I finally convinced him that Ella, who was making eyes at me this season, and me were having a hot affair and I suppose he fell for it since I've been known to play the other side, too. I let Ella in on the secret and so we pretended we were having an affair which was fine until I found out she expected to have a real one . . . you could've knocked me over with a feather when she suggested the idea one afternoon, right after the season opened. I said no and from that time on till she died we were having trouble and I mean *trouble*. She used to do everything she could to break me up on stage and off. I hate to admit it but I was kind of relieved when that cable broke.'

So were a lot of people, I thought, sipping my third coke . . . I was getting more and more wide awake and, perhaps as a result of the caffein I was drinking, more and more keyed up.

Molly, in black satin and a dark wig, joined us. 'Going to make a real night of it, dear?' he asked.

'First real bender this season,' said Louis, looking happy.

'Well, I must say you couldn't pick a better place, and in better company,' said Molly giving me the eye. 'You a dancer, honey?'

I said that I was, in the *corps de ballet*.

'My, they're much more butch than they used to be,' said Molly, turning to Louis. 'What's happened to the mad girls who used to be in your company?'

'Flew away,' giggled Louis. 'Spread their wings and flew away . . . psst! like that, all gone.'

'Well, it's a new look,' said Molly, giving me a tender smile. We had a great deal more to drink and then we left Hermione's. I was wide awake and a little jittery while Louis was roaring drunk, throwing passes almost as fast as I could catch them and throw them back.

At four in the morning we ended up in a Turkish Bath in Harlem. I was very innocent; I figured that if Louis tried to give me a rough time I'd be safe in the baths since they were, after all, a public place with a management which would come to my help if he got too horny. I was mistaken.

144

We undressed in separate lockers, like a beach house, then we went upstairs to the baths: a big swimming pool, then steam rooms and hot rooms and, beyond these, a dark dormitory with maybe a hundred beds in it where you're supposed to lie down and take a nap after your pores have been opened by the heat. Only nobody takes a nap.

Standing by the pool in a strong light, I was very embarrassed not only by what was going on but by Louis who was staring at me, taking inventory. 'Where'd you get those muscles, Baby?' he asked, in a low husky voice.

'Beating up dancers,' I said evenly. But I wasn't too sure of myself. Louis looked like one of those Greek gods with his clothes off, all muscle and perfect proportions, including the bone head. Our presence caused even more of a stir than it had in the different bars. Fat old gentlemen came strolling by; one old fellow could hardly walk he was so old . . . he wheezed and puffed and he looked like a banker, very respectable, very ancient yet here he was, operating like mad, or wanting to.

'Let's go in the steam room,' said Louis and, ignoring the pinches and the pawing, we got through the old gentlemen to the steam room where a number of youths, black and white and tan, were carrying on, dim shapes in the steam which hid everything over a foot away. All around the steam room was a concrete ledge or shelf on which the various combinations disported themselves, doing a lot of things I never thought possible. It was like being in hell: the one electric bulb in the steam room was pink and gave a fiery glow to the proceedings. For the first time that night I was tempted to give up, to run away, to let the whole damned murder case take care of itself. Only the thought of Jane kept me in that steam room.

We climbed up on the ledge out of the way. Louis stretched out beside me while I sat straight up, legs crossed, and he made love noises. It was pretty terrible. Fortunately, he was drunk and not as quick as usual and I was able to keep his hands off me. For several hours I had been trying to clear something up but I couldn't. He was either on to me or else he was too drunk to make sense.

'Come on, Baby, lie down,' he mumbled through the steam as dark shadows moved by us, shadows which would abruptly become curious faces; then, seeing us together, seeing my furious scowl, would recede into the ruddy mist.

'I told you one million times, Louis, I don't like it,' I said in a low voice.

He sat up, his face so close to mine that I could make out the little red veins which edged the bright blue irises of his eyes. 'You don't think I don't know all about you,' he said. 'You think I don't know about Jane?'

'What about Jane?'

'You know as well as I do. Everybody in the company knows . . . no use your trying to bluff.'

'What're you talking about?'

'About Jane and Ella.'

'What about them?'

'Stop looking so dumb . . . Ella had a big thing with Jane, didn't you know that? Just last year. Everybody knew. Ella was crazy for Jane. As long as I knew Ella, Jane was the only person she ever got excited over, except maybe me and that was just because I wouldn't have anything to do with her.'

'I don't believe it.'

'Then go ask Jane . . . she'll tell you. Maybe she'll tell you about the fight they had . . . if she doesn't, the police will.'

2

The sun was shining when I got back to the apartment. I was staggering with fatigue and I was aware of nothing as I fell into bed beside Jane who did not wake up.

Two hours' sleep is not as good as eight but it's better than none. At least I didn't feel that my head was full of feathers when Jane woke me up at ten o'clock.

'What happened to you?' She was already dressed.

I groaned as I sat up shaking the sleep from my eyes. 'Hunting a killer.'

'Did you find one?'

I nodded grimly, wide awake. 'In spite of the fact, nobody's been very co-operative . . . including you.'

'Here's some coffee,' she said, handing me a cup from the table by the bed. Then: 'What do you mean?'

'You and Ella,' I said, looking straight at her. 'I didn't know you went in for that sort of thing.'

She turned very pale. 'Oh my God,' she breathed and sat

146

down with a thump on the bed. 'How did you find out about that?'

'Then it's true?'

'No, not really.'

'It either is or it isn't.'

'Well, it's not. I've been so scared somebody would rake all that business up . . . the police don't know, do they? Gleason didn't tell you, did he?'

'No, I found out from one of the dancers last night. I gather everyone knew about it except me.'

'It's not one of things I most enjoy talking about,' she said with some of her usual spirit.

'I can see why not.'

'And not for the reason you think. It all started about two years ago when Ella needed an understudy in one of the lousy new ballets we were doing then . . . this was before she was such a star: so I was given the job and she offered to teach me the part . . . something which is pretty rare with any dancer but unheard of with someone like Ella. It took me about five minutes to figure it out. From then on, for the next few months, it was something like you and Louis, only worse since I had to work with her. I turned her down a dozen times; then, finally, after being as nice as I could be under the circumstances, I lost my temper and we had a knockdown fight which did the trick: she never bothered me again . . . never spoke to me again as a matter of fact, off stage anyway.'

'Then why does everybody think you were carrying on with her?'

'Because she told them we were, because she got everybody in the company to believe that I was the one who had gone after *her* and that she had been the one who finally threw *me* out.'

'Jesus!'

'That's what I say. Well, even though everybody knew what an awful person Ella was, they tended to believe her since after all, she had so many affairs with men, too, and I wasn't at all promiscuous,' she added primly.

'This may make it kind of tough,' I said, putting on my shirt.

'I don't see why they have to bring all that old stuff up now. What does it have to do with Ella's being killed?'

'Well, they're pretty thorough in these matters, the police

are . . . they'll probably trot out every scandal they can find in the company, if only to make the headlines.'

'I had a premonition about this,' said Jane, gloomily packing her rehearsal bag.

'I wish you'd told me sooner.'

'I was afraid you wouldn't believe me . . . you *do* believe me, don't you?' I gave her a big kiss and we both felt better after that.

'Of course I do. Only a complete hayseed like you could manage to do so many things wrong.'

She shut the rehearsal bag with a snap. 'I almost forgot . . . somebody searched the apartment yesterday.'

'Take anything?'

'Not as far as I could tell.'

'The police . . . probably just a routine checkup.'

'I'll be glad when they make their damned arrest and stop bothering us.'

'That's just because you want to dance Eglanova's roles.'

She smiled wanly. 'I've been wondering, though, who they will get for the rest of the season.'

We took a taxi across town to the studio; we were followed, I noticed, by two plainclothes men in another cab. I said nothing to Jane about this.

Mr. Washburn was at the studio and he greeted me as cordially as ever, as if the unpleasant exchange of the night before had never taken place. 'I hear you were out late,' he said, when I joined him in the reception room, near Madame Aloin's desk. Dancers in tights, detectives, tiny tots, and mothers all milled about. None of the company, though, was in sight.

'How did you know?'

'I saw Louis this morning. He was here for the nine o'clock class.'

'How on earth does he do it? I didn't get to sleep until eight and he was still going strong when I left him.'

'Where were you?'

'In Harlem.'

'Then I suppose he came straight to the class instead of going to bed . . . he often does that when he's been drinking, to sober up.'

'Iron man,' I said, with real admiration. 'Is he still here?'

'He's rehearsing with the rest of the company. How is Jane?'

148

'She doesn't suspect anything.'

'Well, try and keep the papers away from her today. One of them says right out that she's guilty, for personal as well as professional motives.'

'They don't mention her name, do they?'

'No, but they make it clear.'

'I suppose somebody tipped them off about Jane and Ella.'

Mr. Washburn looked solemn but I could see he was pleased. 'So you've found out about that.'

'Yes . . . have the police?'

'Of course. I didn't want to be the one to tell you.'

'Very thoughtful.'

'Yes, I think it *was* thoughtful of me. There was no use in upsetting you with gossip like that. Now that you know, however, I may as well tell you that we're going to have a hard time keeping it out of the trial . . . the state will build its case on that affair, so Bush tells me.'

'When are they going to arrest her?'

'Today, I think; Gleason is in that classroom having a conference. I've told our lawyer to stand by. He's at the office now, waiting. It's terrible, I know, but there's nothing left for us to do but live through it.'

'Have you found someone to take Jane's place in *Eclipse*?'

'No,' said Mr. Washburn emphatically; I knew he was lying.

'Well, don't hire anybody yet . . . don't even write one of those letters of yours.'

He winced slightly at this reference. 'Why not?'

'Because I know who really did the murder.'

He looked like one of those heifers which Alma Shellabarger's old man used to hit over the head with a mallet in the Chicago stockyards. 'How . . . I mean what makes you think you know?'

'Because I have proof.'

'Be very careful,' said Mr. Washburn harshly. 'You can get into serious trouble if you start making accusations you can't back up.'

'Don't worry,' I said, more coolly than I felt. 'I'll be back in an hour.' I was gone before he could stop me.

At the office I ran into Elmer Bush who had somehow got his signals mixed and had expected to meet Mr. Washburn here.

'See the old rag this morning?' he asked brightly, referring to that newspaper which had once given me a berth.

'Too busy,' I said, pushing by him into my office; he followed me.

'Happen to have a copy of it right here,' he said. 'I say in it that there will be an arrest by noon today.'

'Do you say whether the right person will be arrested or not?'

'No, I leave it up in the air,' said Elmer, chuckling.

'You'll find Mr. Washburn over at the studio,' I said coldly, going quickly through the heap of mail on my desk.

'I've got some advice for you, boy,' said Bush, in a serious voice.

'I'm listening.' I didn't look at him; I was busy with the mail.

'Keep out of this. That girl of yours is in big trouble. There're a lot of things you don't know ... just take my word for it. I've been around a long time. I've had a lot more experience dealing with the police ... I know what they're up to. They never act in a big case like this unless they got *all* the dope, unless they're sure they got their suspect signed, sealed and delivered. I like you, Pete; I don't want to see you get torn apart by these wolves. I know you like the girl but there's more in all this than meets the eye ... more than most people, even real friends like Washburn, are willing to tell you.'

I looked up. 'Do you mean to say that I have body odor, Mr. Bush?'

'I was only trying to do you a good turn,' said Elmer Bush, very hurt. He left me alone with my ingratitude.

I looked at my watch; I had less than an hour before the rehearsal broke up, at which time I was fairly sure the arrest would take place. I took out my sheet of paper and went over it carefully: all the mysteries had been solved and the answer to the puzzle was perfectly clear. Short of a confession on the part of the guilty party, however, I was not going to have an easy time proving my case. If worst came to worst, though, I could always announce my theory, get the police to hold up the arrest and then let *them* do the proving, which they could do, in time ... I was sure of that.

I got on the telephone and called an acquaintance of mine at the rival ballet company's office ... he's been the Press agent over there for years. Since we've always been friendly, he told me what I wanted to know ... it helped a little.

It was not until I was out in the street that I recalled I had not shaved or changed my clothes in two days and that I looked incredibly seedy, according to the plateglass window in which I caught an unflattering glimpse of myself. I had not been to my own apartment in several days, not since the afternoon when I had packed my clothes and stormed out of Jane's place.

I let myself in and picked up the suitcase which still lay in the middle of the living-room floor. Then I opened it.

At first I thought someone was playing a joke on me. The bag contained a woman's nightgown, nylon stockings, brassière, panties . . . I examined them all with growing bewilderment. It was not until I discovered the sealed envelope that I realized what had happened, that this was Magda's suitcase.

I had a long talk with Gleason. It lasted for forty minutes and ended just as the rehearsal did, which was good timing for the company was at least able to get through its rehearsal before the killer was arrested.

I purposely held the final bit of evidence back until I had explained, to Gleason's annoyance, how I had put the puzzle together. I'm afraid I was a little smug in my hour of triumph.

'You see,' I said in the same quiet, somewhat bored tone a professor of English I had had at Harvard was accustomed to use with students, 'we all were led astray by the later deaths; we didn't concentrate on the first murder enough, on the character of the murdered woman which was, naturally, the key to the whole business.' I paused in the middle of this ponderous and obvious statement to fix the Inspector with my level gaze, as though I expected him to question what I had said. He didn't. He just looked at me, waiting. His secretary's pencil was poised above his shorthand pad. After a suitable pause, I continued.

'Curiously enough, what I considered to be your somewhat morbid interest in the shears, The Murder Weapon as they are officially called, turned out to be, finally, the first clue I had to the killer's identity; in my pocket I have the final evidence. Between the first clue and the last, however, there is an extremely complex story which I am sure that you never suspected, in its entirety at least . . . I didn't either, I must admit.' I am not sure but I think that at this point, I put the tips of my fingers together.

'Ella Sutton was an ambitious girl, as we all know, and an excellent artist. Her tragedy began (and I think it has all the elements of a classic tragedy: a beautiful, clever, gifted woman rising to glory only to be struck down because of one fatal flaw in her temperament . . . greed).' I was having a very good time; I had shifted now from the slightly bored professor of English to the more suitable role of classic moralist, a Sophocles sitting in judgment. 'Her tragedy, then, began in 1937 when she joined the North American Ballet Company where she met Jed Wilbur, an eager young choreographer, and Alyosha Rudin who, though he was with the present company, was more active in the whole ballet world in those days than he is now. She made, as I construct the case, two friends at that time: Jed, who was not only her choreographer but her political mentor as well, and Alyosha who fell in love with her and, when the North American Ballet folded, was able to take her into this company. Both men had a great influence on her. With Wilbur, she joined the Communist Party . . .'

'You realize what you're saying?'

'Yes, Inspector. They joined the Party and belonged, for a time, to the same cell. Ella, however, was not very much interested in politics, or anything else which didn't help her to get what she wanted professionally . . . she was a true artist when it came to her work: she would do anything to get ahead. I believe she became a Communist to impress Jed, who was indifferent to her sexually; and she became Alyosha's mistress to please him . . . even taking a Russian name for a while in an attempt to make people believe that she was a White Russian born in Paris. All of this you can find in old interviews.

'As you probably know, she quickly lost interest in Alyosha who adored her but cared for the dance more; he refused to push her ahead in the company as fast as she thought she should go. She deserted him finally and married the next most powerful person, from an artistic point of view, Miles Sutton, the conductor. Their marriage was never very happy. She had a bad temper and she was a natural conniver. I suspect much of the trouble she had with the men in her life came from the fact that she was either quite indifferent to sex or else she was, in actual fact, a Lesbian. In any case, she went quickly to the top, and, finally, this season, she got her dearest wish when she prevailed upon Washburn to fire Eglanova. Meanwhile, however, Ella had made a great deal of trouble for herself. She had got involved with Jane Garden in an abortive affair . . . she was genuinely attracted to Jane who is not, contrary to your recent theory, a Lesbian . . . that's one of those things I would know better than you without *any* evidence. And Ella had decided to shed Miles and marry Louis, partly out of attraction (she seemed always to care only for men and women who would have nothing to do with her) and partly because it would be a glamorous marriage or alliance: the king and the queen of ballet.

'Everything might have worked out perfectly if Louis had ever shown the faintest interest in her, but he didn't and there were bitter quarrels. Miles, who now no longer lived with Ella, fell in love with Magda and, as you know, got her pregnant. Even in ballet circles that sort of thing presents a problem and he did his best to get Ella to divorce him. She took it all very lightly . . . it was the sort of thing that amused her and she made it clear that he would have to work his problems out on his own time. I think she was indignant, deep down, that he had preferred another woman to her even though they no longer lived together, even though she despised him . . . naturally, he could have killed her. But he didn't. So, by the time *Eclipse* was to be premièred, Ella had infuriated Miles and Magda, Louis, Mr. Washburn by threatening to leave the company and take Louis with her, Eglanova by succeeding her, Alyosha for deserting him and for getting his beloved Eglanova fired, Wilbur for having blackmailed him into joining the company. . . .

'Now when I had found out all these things, it occurred to me that the person who killed Ella would, naturally, be the one with the most urgent motive or, failing that, the one whose monomania was equal to hers. The most urgent motive was her husband's and I was just as sure as you were that he killed her. But we were all wrong. That left Eglanova, Alyosha, Louis, Wilbur, Mr. Washburn and Jane. I knew Jane hadn't done it. Mr. Washburn, despite a rather sinister nature, had no motive, other than exasperation. Eglanova and Alyosha seemed likely candidates, for nearly the same reason. Louis had no apparent motive. Wilbur had an excellent one.

'Ella needed Wilbur for two reasons: she wanted a modern ballet and she wanted to go into musical comedy. They had grown apart over the years and when she first had Washburn approach him the answer was no. He didn't like the Grand

Saint Petersburg Ballet and he had no intention of leaving his own company, or Broadway. Ella then went to see him and told him, in her definite way, that if he didn't accept Washburn's offer she would give evidence in Washington that he had been, and for all anybody knew now, was still a member of the Communist Party . . . and she had proof. She was the sort of girl who never let go of anything which might one day prove useful. Needless to say, Wilbur joined the company. But like everyone else connected with this mess, he had more than one iron in the fire: you see, he had been in love with Louis for years. Which was, as far as he was concerned, the one good thing about his predicament, about his giving in to Ella.

'Everything might still have turned out all right if Ella had not gone too far and if Louis had been a little brighter. The Grand Saint Petersburg doesn't have much of a reputation for chic but it is a money-maker and Wilbur was allowed a free hand and he did create for Ella what many people think is his best ballet—*Eclipse*. As for Ella's going into musical comedy, well, there was nothing wrong in that either. She could have gotten a job with any management in town on her own . . . so there was no reason why Wilbur shouldn't sponsor her. The complication arose when Ella became interested in Louis, and Louis, who was not at all attracted to Wilbur, used Ella as an excuse for his own coldness, saying that she was the one woman he had ever loved and that they were to be married. Poor Wilbur took this as long as he could. Louis would even pretend to make love to Ella in his dressing room when he knew Wilbur might be within hearing distance.

'This crisis came to a head the afternoon of the day Ella was killed. Wilbur told her he wasn't going to stay in the company another minute, that he was going to break his contract. She told him if he did she would expose him as a Communist and that would be the end of his career. So, believing that he would lose his career as well as his love to Ella, he cut the cable; then he put the shears in Eglanova's dressing room since she seemed as likely a suspect as any.'

I stopped, expecting some outcry from the Inspector, but there was none. 'Go on,' he said.

'Fortunately for Wilbur, Miles was immediately suspected and, as fortunately, Miles died a natural death before he was arrested. The case would have ended there except that Miles had known

154

all along that Wilbur was the real murderer . . . Wilbur never knew that Ella, a very efficient woman, had somehow managed to get hold of his membership card in the Party years ago and, with an eye to the future, had kept it. She was a very shrewd woman . . . the more you study her life the more you have to admire her for the sheer audacity she displayed. If she had been able to identify a bit more with her friends and victims she'd still be alive . . . might even have ended up being adored by everyone like old Eglanova.'

'Why didn't Sutton give us this card?'

'He would if you'd tried to arrest him. He was not rational . . . no man as heavily doped as he was could be. Besides, he must have regarded Wilbur as a benefactor. I do know, though, that he discussed the whole thing with Magda that day he went to Magda's apartment and he either gave her Wilbur's membership card then, or else told her where it was in case something should happen to him. If he didn't give it to her then she could have got it the night she came to his apartment. No matter *how* she got it, the card was in her possession at the time of her death.'

'Why didn't she bring it to us?'

'The same problem . . . why should she? She had nothing against Jed. The death of Ella didn't disturb her one bit and she realized that now with Miles dead the case was over. And it would really *have* been over if, for some reason we may never know, Magda hadn't become suspicious of Jed. She began to think that perhaps Miles had not died naturally. She made a date to talk to him; she told him that she had the Party card and he asked her for it. They were to meet after the rehearsal. I admire the way he went through that rehearsal, not knowing what to expect from Magda who was sitting there with the rest of us on the bench, waiting for him to finish. After the ballet they went into the empty classroom . . . or rather Wilbur joined Magda there after Jane had left her . . . a break for him, the room being empty. She told him that she had the card with her; they quarreled. She demanded to know whether Miles had died naturally or not. There was some sort of scuffle and he grabbed her purse and, either accidentally or on a sudden impulse, he pushed her through the window. Then, taking the card out of her purse, he rushed back into the studio.'

'Then *he* has the card?'

Yes. Magda, however, the day she died came to Jane's apartment as you know, intending to move in. Since the apartment is a small one I was forced to move out . . . which naturally irritated me. So, shortly after Magda arrived, I left . . . after first shoving my own suitcase under the bed and taking hers with me to my own apartment where it remained unopened until an hour ago.'

'What was in that suitcase?'

With a look of quiet triumph I handed Mr. Gleason the photostatic copy Magda had had made of Jed Wilbur's membership card in the Communist Party, dated 1937.

3

It was a blissful evening. I had sold the exclusive story of my apprehension of the murderer to the *Globe* for what is known in the trade as 'an undisclosed amount,' meaning a good deal . . . to the fury of one Elmer Bush whose own story on the arrest of Jane Garden had to be killed at the last minute at great expense, and now Mr. Washburn was entertaining Jane and myself at the Colony Restaurant for dinner.

'You know,' said my erstwhile employer expansively, offering me a cigar, 'though it may sound strange, I always suspected Jed. You remember how I repeatedly maintained that no one connected with my company could have done such a thing? Well, in a sense, I was right . . . it was the newcomer who was responsible, the outsider.'

'Very sound, Mr. Washburn,' I said, glancing at Jane who glowed in coral and black.

'But what made you suspect him . . . when did you get on to him?'

'The evening I went to see him in his apartment and tried to get him to talk about the murder. At first he wouldn't, which was suspicious. But then, after much coaxing, he did suggest that perhaps Eglanova had done the murder and then put the shears in her own dressing room to make herself appear victimized. Well, I knew that only three people in the company knew where those shears had been found originally . . . you, Eglanova and myself. Only the murderer could have known that they had been
156

placed in her wastebasket because it was the murderer who had put them there. Very simple.'

'Isn't he wonderful?' sighed Jane. I preened myself.

'Now isn't that remarkable,' said Mr. Washburn with a gentle smile.

'Remarkable?'

'Why, yes. You see I told Wilbur about those shears . . . or rather I mentioned it to Eglanova in Wilbur's presence. I felt at that time it would make no difference since the case seemed solved . . . Miles was dead and the police were satisfied. I must say it was fortunate, all in all, that you were able to locate Wilbur's Party card. Otherwise he would have said that he'd learned about those shears from me.'

'That may be,' I said evasively, feeling a little sick to my stomach. 'Anyway, it's all over and he's confessed.'

'*And* you did a bang-up job,' said Mr. Washburn, riding high on the wind he had knocked from my sails. 'Not only did you save this little lady from an unpleasant experience but you have cleared the whole company of these crimes. I am more grateful than I can say.'

To this tribute, I made chivalrous answer.

'We are also fortunate that the arrest didn't take place earlier because now, I am happy to say, the new ballet is in good enough shape for the Chicago opening. A real bit of luck under the circumstances. It'll be a sensation . . . the *Murderer's Ballet* . . . I can see the papers now.'

Reflecting sadly that the Ivan Washburns of this world always win, Jane and I went home to celebrate. A row of Miss Flynn's asterisks could alone describe our bliss.

Strong Poison

by Dorothy L. Sayers

"The prisoner had the means—the arsenic. She had the expert knowledge, and she had the opportunity to administer it." The judge's summing-up was clear. Harriet Vane was guilty. And Harriet Vane should hang. But the jury disagreed . . .

It left Lord Peter Wimsey four short weeks to prove that Harriet Vane had not murdered her lover with arsenic, and to find the real murderer. It appeared an impossible task. The Crown's case was watertight; the police were adamant that the right person was on trial.

Only Peter Wimsey stood between Harriet Vane and the gallows.

FOUR  **SQUARE EDITION 3s. 6d.**

The Mists of Fear

by John Creasey

She was beautiful, and in her red dress she was the most conspicuous thing in sight. A light mist gathered round her —and she was gone. Near the place where she was standing a molten pit appeared. Incredible; yet there were a dozen witnesses who saw it happen.

Dr. Palfrey, working on the case, finds that he is pitted against an enemy who can kill silently, swiftly and anonymously. His life is in danger—and perhaps even the fate of the world hangs in the balance.

FOUR ◢◣ SQUARE EDITION 2s. 6d.